Outliving the Undead

First in the Walker Series

Zelda Davis Lindsey

This is a work of fiction. Names, characters, places, and incidents either are the product of the author's imagination or are used fictitiously. Any resemblance to actual persons, living or dead, events, or locales is entirely coincidental.

Copyright © 2010 by Zelda Davis Lindsey

All rights reserved. No part of this book may be reproduced or used in any manner without written permission of the copyright owner except for the use of quotations in a book review. For more information, address:zeldavis@yahoo.com

First paperback edition August 2022

Book design by Zelda Davis Lindsey

DEDICATION

Dedicated to my family for without their love and support this book would have remained only in my memory.

CHAPTER 1

The zombie froze the same time I did, not five feet away. My heart was racing, and my mind kept repeating, Crap, Crap, Crap.

I had rounded the corner without checking and almost ran into the walker. The stench rising from it brought bile to my throat, and the rotting flesh hanging in strips from its stinking body swayed after it had stopped. It was a female, as one breast was visible, swaying heavily each time it moved. Tilting its head, it leaned toward me a bit and sniffed. It tilted its head back and forth, gave a little nort, turned, and shuffled away.

I would've been offended if I hadn't been so damned scared. I glanced down at myself as if I could see what offended it, then I shook my head and sighed.

Nope, it wasn't me. I haven't had a bath in a bit, but I used the hell out of baby wipes and sprayed myself with some Scent be Gone used by hunters to conceal their scent while hunting, so that must of been the reason it hadn't smelled fresh meat. It ambled away, listing sharply to one side, which caused it to bump repeatedly into the building until it rounded the corner and disappeared. Walkers had been with us for about 6 months now. Hundreds of stories were circulating about what caused them, but I don't think anyone knew. The religious leaders had a field day with it, saying it was the wrath of God. But I knew God was a gentle, caring, and loving God, and He would never put this on His people.

I stood there, knowing I needed to move but unable to get my body to do more than breathe in and out. I finally braced my hand against the hot, brick building and dragged great big breaths of humid East Texas air into my lungs until my mind cleared enough to tell me to move. I started to stumble past the front of the building when I heard a soft "whoosh" to my left. I slowly turned my head towards the noise and stared in stunned disbelief as the door opened... automatically. I could feel the cool air that rushed out and was drawn almost magically into the store.

It was a pet store. One of those that provided designer suits and glitzy what-knots for your pet. It was a strange store for this little Texas town, but you never know what you'll find any more. It was not my choice of buildings to look for supplies, but what the hell? I was here, so I might as well look.

I had to carry a backpack to leave my gun arm free. I don't use a gun much anymore. I use a cross-bow because it's quieter. It took me several weeks to get the hang of it because of the "thunk" it made when it went into a walker's head. The ick factor was way off the shudder scale, and I had tried to ignore it, but damn, it was what it was...a quiet way to kill and not attract a herd of walkers when you only needed to kill one. I tried to pull the arrow out of a walker's head once, but it didn't work for me when the brains started coming out. Needless to say, I go through a lot of arrows. I had a quiver of arrows attached to each thigh, and the bow had a holder built in that held eight arrows. An infrared camera hung off my belt, which allowed me to see the

heat signatures of the walkers in the dark. All the added weight is why I've lost so much weight and finally slimmed down. Muscles took over for the fat, and I felt like I'd sweat off five pounds daily in the heat and humidity. The world had to go to hell for me to start looking good; now, there

wasn't anyone to care
The story of my life.
I took out the infrared camera and scanned the area. I was alone, at least in the front of the store. I quickly searched the back and used the restroom while I was there. I walked to the checkout counter and collapsed on the top bag of a stack of 50-pound dog food. The cool air made the sweat on my skin thicken and my short, red hair stick to my forehead. Again, I sighed at
the thought of a hot shower as I tugged at the back of my tee shirt to free it from my sweat-soaked skin. Some dreams just keep returning.
Taking a deep breath, I got up and began to rummage under the counter for batteries. We never had enough batteries because everything we had needed every size of batteries. For some reason, we had trouble finding a D cell. I found one of those foot-long flashlights and was busy tucking it in my backpack when I heard the soft rush of the door again and dropped down behind the counter. That's when it hit me...electricity!! Automatic doors! Air conditioning! What was I thinking? The sound of footsteps slowly approached the counter and then stopped. A male voice above me said, "Don't you think we should

do something about those doors? No telling what might walk in off the street."

I looked up and saw the silhouette of a man with a backpack, or at least I hoped it was. He was back lit and looked like a big black man-shaped blob. With my luck, it was the Hunch Back of Notre Dame since my luck had been running on the crappy side for a few months.

"Shit," I said, "Who the hell are you?" I noticed I was still a little shaky from the encounter on the street, or I would have thought about turning off the doors myself. It's not like I'm brain dead like the rest of the town, just a bit unnerved. Really!!

I began to look around the counter area for something that looked like a switch or whatever it took to turn off the doors when the sound of a car alarm started going off about a block away. We looked quickly at each, then, like we'd been shot in the ass, frantically began to look for the off switch to the doors before they opened and admitted a herd of walkers. After a harried moment of looking, the black blob sprinted to the back of the store, and a few moments later, the air conditioning went quiet. He'd shut off the main switch. If he hadn't beaten me to the punch, I'd thought of doing that.

He started back to the front of the store, stopped abruptly, put his finger to his lips, and motioned to the door. I ducked behind a display of cat toys as a walker scuffled past the door towards the alarm. The doors remained closed. Soon a procession of walkers slowly made their way past the store and down the street towards the noise. They liked noise. The louder, the better; gunshots, door slams, breaking glass, car alarms, and here they came. Mouths gaping, arms swinging, eyes unblinking and shuffling along. I saw a couple of them run once, but they mostly shuffle. I've seen a herd of walkers gathered around wind chimes for days. Yep, wind chimes were a real crowd pleaser for sure. I vowed to never own another one.
Bright and shining were next on their list of likes. Flares, flashlights, headlights, fires, and reflections yell 'lunch' for the undead. As I waited for the procession of the dead to wander down the street to eat the car, I secretly examined my new friend. Just a bit taller than my 5'7", his muscular form carried a backpack over one shoulder. I couldn't carry one that way, as it kept slipping off. His long, wavy, dark-colored hair was sweaty and stuck to his forehead. He smelled sweaty and

male. Yep, I was interested.

I searched for batteries and flashlights (you never seem to have enough flashlights) and finally found a switch marked "doors."

Motioning to my new best friend, he disappeared into the back, and sweet air filtered back on. I swiftly flipped the switch to the "off" position and crossed my fingers. Then I worked my way to the back of the store.

He was standing near a window and motioned me over to him. We saw a group of about 30 walkers milling around the screeching car, bumping it repeatedly. "Names Mason," he whispered, "I thought you'd bought it back there."

"Yeah, me too," I replied quietly. "I'm J.D."

I'd been chased from one end of this town to the other by the undead and a group of motorcycle riders, so being comfortable around a stranger was new for me. Since I was always being chased from one of this town to the other, it allowed me to figure out where most of the stores were located.

I set up experiments to see what drew the dead, like dead animals. Nope, they had to be kicking. They stuck up their noses to perfume. Their preferred raw meat to cooked meat. I lost a lot of weight, nearly wet myself a few times, and repeatedly learned where my gag reflex was. Mason moved quietly and seemed very sure of himself. I enjoyed watching him move and had to shake myself to get back on track. I thought about peeking into his mind, but just because you're a telepath doesn't mean you should go around reading people's minds.

When I was small and still learning, I received a lot of information I still can't get rid of. Sometimes, if someone is a strong sender, you get stuff anyway. It just happens. I did find out I can't read the walkers. There is nothing there, I guess.

"What did you come in here for?" he asked.

"What did you come here for?" I asked at the same time.

You first," we both said.

I held a hand to quiet him and motioned him away from the window. Before I could say anything, a low buzzing sound came from my backpack. Holding up my finger in the universal sign of "just a minute," I started digging through my pack for my walkie and said quietly, "I'm fine, wait a minute."

To Mason, I said, "The others would have heard the car alarm and are wondering if I'm ok, so I need to take this. If you're one of "The Three Musketeers" chasing us for the last month, you should know we change the codes regularly. Understood?" He frowned slightly, definitely not understanding, and finally said, "Go for it," and walked back to the front of the store.

I walked over to a display of dog collars and pressed the mike button. "The tree has lost its leaves," then I smiled and said, "Mercy has a brand new shoe." In other words, I'm on my way back, and I have a surprise for you, so be ready. If I had to take Mason back with me, then the others won't be surprised by him and would be waiting armed and ready.

We had been followed and harassed for over a month by these three fools on motorcycles. They rode around on Harley's and wore black. There are so many things wrong with this picture I don't know where to start. Harley's are loud, so the fools were usually followed by a procession of crazy walkers. The black clothes? Well, really? in Texas? in July? I'm surprised they've survived as long as they have but not surprised they were after us. We have food and arms....something they want but are too lazy to get on their own. I mean, really, it's free. Just go get it. Sheesh! I don't know if Mason is involved with the group, but it's best to be prepared. I also wasn't sure how dangerous these nutcases were, so we were cautious.

"Well, as much as I hate to leave this wonderful cool store, I need to get back. You are welcome to join us if you're not part of the Stupid Squad or trying to rob us. We don't play fair, though, so be warned. If you try anything, you will die. Understood?"

"Perfectly." His smile lit up the world, then he turned toward the door and came face to face with a walker. Sure there was a door between them, but it didn't lessen the heart attack. "Shit," he muttered, then stumbled back into a display of dental products for pets.

After he settled down and I managed not to laugh, we both headed for the back of the building at a run while the walker beat on the front door. Mason paused long enough to shut down the electricity, and I gave a thumbs up to the action. If we don't get air conditioning, they don't either.

I loaded my bow at the back door while Mason checked the alley. We slowly crept out, and when he started to turn left, I tapped his shoulder, making him jump a foot, and motioned to the right. He blushed, then shrugged and headed in that direction. Near the street, there was a dumpster we hid behind while I indicated to him with hand signals that we needed to go right for two blocks and then left on the next block.

He gave a thumbs up, looked around the dumpster, and ran to the corner of the building. He looked both ways before he motioned me up to him, and we began the exciting but uneventful trip back to the library we were using for home base. When we arrived, I stopped him in the alley and pointed at the fire escape stairs. Grabbing a bent pipe that I kept near the side of the building, I reached up, snagged the bottom stair, and pulled it down. He ran up the stairs, and when I got to the landing, I pulled them back up and secured them with a piece of a chain so they couldn't be pulled back down. I had used axel grease I had found at an auto parts store to make sure the stairs were quiet.

When we got to the roof, I led him to the hatch, bent down, and knocked three times. Metal rubbing on metal indicated it was being unlocked, and then it opened, and a small figure appeared. "Hurry," they said. "The Stupid Squad is coming." We hurried down the ladder, and just before I closed the hatch, I heard the unmistakable sound of motorcycles. Shaking my head, I locked the hatch and followed Mason as he was led back to the library reading room.

He stopped in the doorway, so I quietly said, "Excuse me," and gently pushed past him into the room.

The library's reading room was at the center of the building. Stacks of books filled rooms on three sides with the checkout desk and reference room in the front. Each door was locked for safety, with the librarian's office to the rear of the reading room with an attached bath on one side and a closed door to a stairway leading upstairs to the rooftop. It was our way in and out of the building unseen.

The reading room itself boasted three large sofas and a fireplace. We slept on the sofas and could use lanterns with the doors closed. I had a stack of plastic tubs filled with books on Medicine, gardening, sewing, raising livestock, first aid, computer science, etc.

I went out daily and collected every arrow, shaft, and tip I could find, along with MRE (meals ready to eat) from the local Army/Navy store. I had tried the local Walmart store, but as usual, it was crowded but not with the living. I ended up at the mom-and-pop stores and convenience stores. Bottle water, medical supplies, drugs such as asthma inhalers (for me), and antibiotics were also on the list. The survival books told me what to do, and I had been swamped. Once I figured I knew as much as I needed (or wanted) to about walkers, I spent most of my time closeted in the library reading survival books and magazines. A "Zombie Survival Guide" was printed before the walkers appeared. It was a work of fiction, but much of it was relevant. I bet reality was a shock for the author.

I shared the library with my sister, Lacy. She's 16, fulfilling every horror story I had ever heard about teenagers. She was a pretty, doe-eyed cheerleader back home. Tall and thin like most girls her age, she somehow made it work for her. She has a high forehead and square chin, thanks to dad, but the button nose, supple lips, and big brown eyes were all mom. It worked well for her, although there wasn't anyone to appreciate it. We were coping and trying to remain upright in the process. So far, so good.

Our mom, dad, and Lacy lived in Florida when the virus hit. I lived in Montana but went down to Florida to keep her company while they were on vacation in Italy. The plane crashed into the ocean on the return flight. It took us several days to make it this far, only because Howard rescued us when our pickup truck died. He was driving the fanciest tow truck I have ever seen. I had plans to get myself a new truck from the local dealership on the other side of town but then thought an RV would be a better way to go. I don't have to worry about paying for it anymore, right? Might as well go for it.

"Everyone, this is Mason. He's a cool head in an emergency, doesn't argue, and has a weird sense of humor. Mason, the gang. I need to change clothes. Lacy, I need to talk to you."

Leaving the room, I walked into the office and the bathroom. Turning on the battery-powered lantern, I started disrobing and reached for the baby wipes. Cleaning off the Scent Be Gone and a lot of the sweat, I changed into new clothes(we didn't have a washer and dryer) and smiled at the cute teenager in the mirror.

"Man, that is one fine piece of man-flesh if I have ever seen one," she sighed, then put down the toilet lid and sat on it. "Where did you find him, and can I have him?

"You have never seen a fine piece of man flesh in

your life, and no, you can't have him. No matter how badly you want to play with him, he isn't a toy." The baby wipe felt terrific on the back of my neck.

"Wow, big surprise there." She started playing with the fringe of her shirt. "Before you ask, Duke is monitoring the Leathernecks, and he said they went on by. What did you bring back other than the God of all gods."

After running a brush through my short hair, I turned toward the sink, fished out two bottles of water, and started back to the office, with Lacy following closely. "I found two more flashlights, D cell batteries, and a huge box of candy bars. It is hotter than Hades and getting hotter, so I don't know what kind of condition they're in."

Walking into the reading room, I handed a bottle of water to Mason, who was sitting comfortably on the couch with one leg crossed at the knee and one arm slung across the back. He smiled, opened the bottle, and took a deep drink. Saluting me with the bottle, he glanced around the room and examined Lacy closely.

"This is Lacey. She's 16 years old and my sister. Any questions?" The room was quiet as everyone watched the stranger.

"They all related to you or just her?"

"Just her. Duke, over there is our tech officer. The pretty lady next to him is Sarah, his wife. She was a corporate lawyer in Atlanta before the walkers and a damned fine cook. She waved the spoon in the air at that. Hiding behind her is Mandy. She doesn't have much to say. We found her hiding in a storage shed. Howard, our mechanic, is getting things ready so we can leave in the morning. He should be back soon."

Mandy peeked around Sarah, smiled at Mason, and quickly hid again. She was a dirty little thing when we found her. How she managed to survive as long as she had surprised us. Skinny and smelling to high heaven, we were delighted to find a blond-haired, blue-eyed little girl under all that grime. She slept for two days after we finally filled her belly. She had attached herself to Sarah and Duke, and they were happy to have her.

Mason nodded to the ladies, got up and shook Duke's hand, smiled at Mandy, then turned to me as we walked to the other side of the room.

Duke and Sarah was a happy encounter, although he nearly scared the crap out of me. He was hiding inside a dryer at an appliance store. Since Duke is a little person and too short to see me over the appliances, he hid when he heard me coming. When I walked by, he knocked on the glass till he got my attention, then grinned like a Cheshire cat when I bent to look inside. He is also crazy about Hawaiian shirts. He brought Sarah back to the library to meet us; we've been together ever since."You say you're leaving in the morning. Mind my asking where you're going. Not that it matters, I've been doing ok on my own, but I recognize that there is safety in numbers, and where ever you're going is fine with me. I'm sick and tired of being tired, and the company of others is a welcome relief. If you'll have me, I'm a good carpenter, scavenger, and all-around handyman, and I'm not afraid of work either."

"It's a democratic society here, Mason. We'll talk about it together and decide. We may have a few questions for you; you can't blame us, and I know I do. So if you're willing to do your share, we'll talk after we eat.

"What about this, Howard? Won't he have something to say about it?"

"Of course, we'll ask him when we see him. But he may not
 return until the morning, and if it gets too crowded, he may just spend the night where he

is."

"Soups on everybody," called Sarah from a corner of the room where a makeshift kitchen had been erected. A small outdoor grill had a large pot of stew bubbling away, and we placed it next to the doorway leading upstairs so it would be ventilated. Next to that were plastic silverware, some more water bottles, and several containers of Crystal Light. A box of crackers rounded out the meal, and the newly acquired box of soft, warm candy bars would be the dessert. Everyone helped themselves.

After the meal, Mason took himself off to the bathroom while the group discussed him. They all knew I was telepathic and wanted my opinion, and I told them that he was ok, so they decided he could join the group. When he returned, they all smiled and welcomed him.

"What about Howard?" he asked.

"What about him?" asked Howard.

Mason turned and saw a tall man of about 50 walking in the door, wiping his hands on a dirty towel, followed closely by Lacy. He had a white mustache and goatee and was of medium build. Howard glanced at him and smiled as he walked to the kitchen and accepted a bowl of stew from

Sarah after removing a black, floppy cowboy hat and putting it on the lampshade. Then he turned, raised his eyebrows at Mason, looked at me, and winked.

"Well, it seems the group has decided I can stay, and you were the only one who hasn't had a say in it."

"So it matters what I have to say?" Howard said, then drank half a bottle of water.

Mason looked at everyone, then at Howard.

"Yeah, it matters. I won't stay if you don't want me here. You want me to leave? I'll leave right now if you want."

I shook my head and started to say something when Howard grinned and sat on the couch, balancing the bowl of stew and placing the water bottle on the floor between his feet. "Naw, if it's ok with the rest of these fine folk, then it's fine with me. But she knew that", nodding towards me, "or she wouldn't have brought ya back with her. She is smart, has a good sense of people, and ain't got no one kilt so far. I trust her; we all do. Now let me finish this fine meal."

Lacy helped Sarah with the cleanup. Duke and I checked out the supplies I had brought back. Howard finished his meal, thanked Sarah, and went into the restroom. Bubba, his part weenie and part chihuahua dog, followed him inside. Where one went, the other was sure to follow. Howard sticks Bubba into a bag and hangs him over his shoulder when we are in a hurry. He had taught Bubba not to bark, but that little dog could growl if there was trouble nearby. They were one gutsy pair.

 they emerged from the restroom, Howard was cleaned up and in a new pair of bib overalls. I hated the things, but I have never seen him in anything else. His ratty old cowboy hat had a snakeskin band with an eagle feather stuck on one side. He gently placed it over the lampshade near the head of his pallet, then he lay down and began to snore. Everyone just smiled. Mandy got two bowls and put water in one and dog kibbles in the other for Bubba. He ate, drank water, and then turned in three small circles before he curled beside Howard. Soon he was snoring too.

"You got a ride, Mason?" I asked, sitting on the couch and removing my Nikes. Lacy found a few blankets and a pillow and made a pallet for Mason. Mason watched Lacy for a minute, nodded his thanks, and started removing his boots.

"Yeah, I have a motorcycle and trailer locked up

in a storage shed down the block. It's fueled up and ready to go." The sound of motorcycles intermittent in the distance and the faint sound of a car alarm made me realize how much I missed the quiet.

"We'll pick it up on our way out of town in the morning." He nodded, then lay down on his pallet. I lay down on the sofa and turned the lantern off. I thought sleep would be hard to find, but I was out before I knew it.

CHAPTER 2

The morning started with a lot of moaning (from the living) and the wonderful smell of coffee. Mason stumbled off to the restroom, looking bedraggled and cute. Breakfast consisted of pop tarts with orange juice. I was the type of person who grumbled and mumbled until I had some coffee. Give me coffee, or I give you death. Everyone deserves to have a vice. That was mine. If I had to eat another pop tart, I'd shoot myself in the head with my cross-bow.

When Mason arrived, Sarah handed him a cup of coffee and a pop tart. Sipping the coffee, he watched with interest the comings and goings of the group. Quietly, our things were packed into plastic totes and taken downstairs, stacked near the alley door. Mason downed his coffee and helped, picking up a tote of books. His grunt when he lifted the heavy tote made Howard smile, but he never said anything. When everything was gone, I left, pulling the door closed and thanking the gods for the sanctuary.

Howard and Duke had taken four pieces of plywood and painted what the alley looked like from each end, making a false wall. The plywood sits about five feet apart, allowing us to move from one building to another unseen. After we'd transferred everything, the door was padlocked from the inside. There was a collective sigh of relief heard in the cavernous building.

Standing in the dark, we could make out the shapes of our outfits. It was a large warehouse filled with one RV, one school bus, and the largest wrecker I have ever seen. Of course, it belonged to Howard. When Mason gave me a questioning look, I mouthed. Don't ask. I still shook my head when I saw it. It was painted desert camouflage so was the RV and the school bus. He had gotten very excited with the spray paint. We couldn't go near the place for two days until the paint dried. Mason took it in and shook his head.

The RV was mine, brand new, of course, with solar panels and two pullouts. Duke claimed the school bus. He and Howard were loading the bus with the totes. Duke had built a bed behind the driver's seat, and all computer monitors with computers anchored to the floor underneath. The other end is where Sarah's treadle sewing machine and dozens of bolts of Hawaiian material were located. He had trouble finding shirts he liked in his size, so she made them for him.

He'd fashioned an air conditioner on the roof, and inside, a plastic curtain divided the bus from the storage area. That way, he only cooled the room where they were. At night he moved the plastic back a bit, and the air conditioner cooled that area too.

The wrecker was Howard's and Bubba's and was painted a sickening green color when he got it. The camouflage was a vast improvement, and it sported a sleeper and a small refrigerator fancy CB and TV. Mason looked around and said, "Why haven't the motorcycle nuts found this?"

I smiled. "Because Lacy made a new sign for the building. It reads 'Lacey's Diaper Service.'"

He laughed and looked at Lacy, giving her a big smile and two thumbs up.

"Now what?"

"Now the fun begins."

Howard and Bubba got into the wrecker and settled in. Duke, Sarah, and Mandy settled in the school bus, with Duke at the wheel. Lacy and I belted ourselves in and rolled the windows down.

Mason stood there uncertainly, trying to figure out where to go.

"If you would open the garage doors, you can jump into the school bus till we get to your storage shed." he nodded and stood ready to open the doors.

"I got em on signal now, J.D," Duke said, staring at the screen of his small laptop. He'd put homing devices on each of the Loonie's motorcycles so we could keep track of them since they tended to show up at the oddest times.

"They're still at the manor house. Must be too early for them."

"Well, they are about to get a rude awakening. I'm ready when you are, Duke." He nodded, raised his mike, turned it up, and yelled, "Mayday, Mayday, Mayday. I've had a flat tire, and you must come BACK and get me." He yelled into the mike.

I yelled at him on my mike, "I told you not to use this channel, you twit." Duke winced at that, then smiled and replied, "I don't care what you said, I'm broken down, and you can't leave me here. You have to come BACK and help me."

We waited for a minute while Duke studied the computer screen, then he gave a thumbs up and a big smile indicating the Goon Squad was moving out.

"OK, I'll send Howard back for you, and we'll meet up at the rest area north of Jackson. Just stay off this channel till then."

"Ten-four." Duke replied into the mike, and after a few tense moments, he laughed and yelled, "They went for it. Let's go."

Mason opened the garage doors, then jumped into the open doorway of the bus, where he rode till we arrived at the storage area where he kept his bike and trailer. It was a pretty black Honda Goldwing. He had several plastic totes on the trailer and a camouflage tarp wrapped tightly around them. I thought that was a good idea and was determined to remember to get a few of them as soon as possible.

The caravan then headed west. We avoided as many towns as possible, driving down dusty roads, but there were times we had no choice but to go down the middle of town. We quickly learned that the herds of walkers congregated in areas of the big stores rather than downtown. Howard would position his wrecker in front and smack the walkers if they got in the way. It wasn't a pretty sight, but it worked. The big stores were at either end of town. So we had to take several

shortcuts.
The weather remained sunny and hot. The trees and scrub started to thin out. We were in tall pines, but the land was beginning to roll, and we lost more grass. The dessert would be coming soon, and less civilization meant fewer walkers. We were cool inside the RV, and I tried not to feel sorry for Mason on his fancy motorcycle, but I thought a bit of sympathy wouldn't hurt if he didn't know about it.

The scenery changed significantly during the morning. Starting from tall pines, we saw more flat, naked land and a lot of dirt. Near noon and north of Waco, I signaled Mason to pull over into a vacant lot next to a filling station. When we settled, we gathered in the RV, drinking cool water and pop from the fridge.

"Duke, do we have anything on the where bouts of the Triplets"?

"They went off the computer screen about an hour after we left this morning. They were headed north at a pretty good clip, so we won't have to worry about them anymore."

"I don't know. They are stupid and lucky enough to stumble upon us when we least expect it, so let's pretend they are still following us for a few more days."

"Works for me," he said, then took a deep swallow of the pop.

"Mason, what do you when it rains?" I asked as I flipped the sliced spam in the skillet.

"I usually just hole up somewhere. The last time I tried to run in the rain, I took out a walker cause I couldn't see through the rain on my face shield. I banged up my ride and had to find another. I lucked out on the Goldwing, but I don't ride when the roads are wet. Why?"

"We must fix it so we can haul your stuff when the weather turns nasty. That way, we can keep going. You OK with that?"

"I got a hitch on the wrecker, and there's one on the bus. Why don't we look out for another trailer." Howard said.

"Why don't I just get a truck, and I could put my stuff in the back and the bike on the trailer? The trailer has a set of ramps, so I'll be good to go. I'll keep an eye out since we won't be seeing rain for a bit, and when I find a truck that will do, I'll load the cycle up and go. But who wants to drive the truck when I'm on the cycle?" Mason asked as he washed his hands in the sink.

"Lacy can drive if you don't mind. What about

you, Lacy, Are you willing to drive his truck when he's on the cycle? Might get a bit lonesome for you."

"Long as it has a CD player and some tunes, I'll be fine. I'll need a walkie, tho, so I know what y'all are doing."

"OK, we got that figured out. Do you want to keep going or hunker down here for the night? It's up to you."

Everyone looked at each other and shrugged their shoulders.

"OK, well, why don't we plan to leave here in about an hour? That will get us farther down the road. Then we stop before dark."

After a short meal, the guys went to the gas station and pilfered what they could. Out came several bags of potato chips and dip. Nibbling on the chips, everyone settled in then we were on the road again. I wanted to get onto the interstate as these two-lane roads were too easily blocked.

We'd gone quite a ways when I noticed Mason racing back towards us from around the corner, so I stopped and rolled down my window. The blast of hot, humid air nearly took my breath away as Mason stopped by my window. His sweat-soaked hair stuck to his face, and he shook like a dog to dislodge it so he could see me.

"We got a fine roadblock ahead. It's on a bridge, and there is no way we'll get through there. We have to find another route."

"I saw a rocky road back about two miles. Maybe it would take us around the roadblock." I got up, went to the table, and spread the road map on top. Mason came in, went to the tiny fridge, and removed a water bottle. Soon, everyone was milling around the RV. Duke climbed up on top to keep watch as we tried to figure out what road to take.

Suddenly, there were three short raps on the roof. We squatted down to look out the front window and saw a herd of walkers approaching us. We quickly rolled up the windows, locked the doors, shut off the engine, and closed the curtain on the rear window. Howard quietly stepped out and took Mandy and Sarah with him. I saw Howard, who was directly behind us, slipping Mandy and Sarah into his truck, closing the door, and with a nod at us, getting into the bunk and closing the curtain.

We knew Duke would be OK on top as long as he stayed down, and since we didn't have the time to get him inside, we had no choice but to leave him there. I knew he hated the walkers enough to be glued to the RV's roof.

We waited in the gathering heat quietly, but the tension was thick enough to cut. Lacy rocked gently back and forth., her way of dealing with it. A concerned Mason looked at her, then back at me. I shook my head and gave him a thumbs up. She'd be OK. She was good that way.

Occasionally there was a slight rocking motion as the walkers would bump into us. Once there was an attempt to open the door, but only briefly. Just enough to make you want to wet yourself. Soon all was quiet, and then two fast knocks on the roof.

When no one moved to open the door, there was a knocking similar to a shave and a haircut, two bits.

Mason chuckled and glanced out the window before he opened the door and admitted a pale, sweaty Duke.

"Water," he croaked and collapsed into the chair. Lacy got him a water bottle while I started the RV and air conditioning.

"Well," I said, "that makes the day memorable."

"Any more memorable, and I'll just shit my pants," he said and finished the water. "Let me know what you decide. I need to check on the girls." Out the door, he went.

"OK, let's go back to that gravel road. It looks like from the map, it crosses the bridge and then meets the highway about 10 miles down. What do you think?

Mason looked at the map while slowly rubbing the cool water bottle across his forehead.

"Why don't I take the bike and check it out just in case it's blocked? I wouldn't want to run into that herd with no way to turn around."

"You sure you want to do that? The road is there, so there must be farms along the way. If we have to turn around, we should be able to find a place. It's up to you, but it was just a thought."

"Let me talk to the others and see what they have to say, but we need to do something other than watch walkers walk by. We can't go forward, so we need to do something. Besides, I don't think Duke could take it."

"Go ahead, and I'll look at the map and see what I can figure out."

Mason left, and Lacy sat staring out the window.

"You OK, kiddo?" I asked quietly.

"I'm tired of all this crap, sis. I know everyone else is, too but damn, when does it end? I'm always scared, and I want a shower, a bowl of ice cream, and the nightly news." I gently caressed her shoulder but couldn't think of a thing to say. We have had this conversation numerous times, and there just wasn't much left to say.

"I don't know about the nightly news, kiddo, but I'm working on the rest of it. I want the same things except for maybe a bubble bath and large hamburger with everything but pickles still; we'll get by."

"I know, thanks." she sniffled, then got up and went to the bathroom.

Just then, Mason returned. "They say take the road and see what happens. They don't want to wait and see if the walkers come back. Duke is still shaking, and the girls were pretty shaken up. Doing anything at this time would be better than sitting here."

"You gonna be OK on the bike?"

He looked up the road at the roadblock, grinned, and said, "I'll be right back ."Then he got on his bike and took off down the road. When Lacy returned from the bathroom, I asked her to tell everyone else we were turning around and returning to the rock road.

Howard was in front of Duke and the bus, so I

figured it would take a few minutes to get us back down the road two miles.

We had just gotten to the gravel road when I noticed a pickup with a motorcycle on a trailer headed our way. I grinned as I realized Mason had gotten himself a new ride. It was an extended cab, double duty, dual tires, macho, everything. Yep, it suited him just fine. He led the way down the road, the land flat, mostly sand with scrub oak. The road was pretty good, and we made pretty good time. Around a curve ahead, we saw an old two-story farmhouse. We stopped and stared at the gate. It was covered in more warning signs than I'd ever seen in one place. Just then, an old man stepped out from behind a slanted, weathered, old shed with the biggest gun I've ever seen in my life. It was pointed at Mason. He did look meaner than the rest of us, but still.

"Keep on going. You ain't welcome here." He shouted, bringing the rifle to his shoulder and sighting down the barrel. His hair was dirty and hairy, which went well with the scraggly beard and teeth so green I could see what was left of them. I could swear I could smell him and wrinkled my nose at the thought. "We intend to, mister, but we were wondering if the road ahead is clear," Mason shouted. "It's clear, git." He motioned the gun toward it and swung it back on Mason again. Mason slowly began moving down the road, with the rest of us taking up the rear. Lacy said that dirty old man stood there "pointing that canon at us" until she couldn't see him anymore.

The bridge was a nightmare. It looked like it was built during the Spanish-American War. Several floorboards were broken, leaving significant holes on the floor, and I could swear it swayed while we were on it. We decided to take it one at a time. By the time we got back to the highway, we were all exhausted.

Mason pulled up behind an abandoned convince store, and we assembled beside him. It reminded me of the circling of the wagons at the end of the day, like in the old westerns, but we didn't park one behind the other, just next to each other so we could leave quickly without being stuck behind someone.

"OK, that's it, I'm done. It's been a long day, but we have made good time. Still, I can't move another inch." Sarah seconded the motion and began to throw some grub together. Mason saw a concrete water tank next to a windmill full of warm water. That started a lottery to see who got the first bath and who got to hold the curtain.

I was at the table examining the map when Howard and Bubba came in, ruffled my hair, got a bowl down, and poured some of his water in it for Bubba.

"Right, interesting day, but I'm glad it's done. Bubba said he didn't need any more drama and was hitting the sack early. I think he might be right, so we will grab a pop tart and head back. Are you planning an early morning, kiddo"?

"Think so. I want to be headed north tomorrow at this time. We should be seeing less civilization by noon at least."

"We could handle that, couldn't we, Bubba? Come on, boy, let's find a nice tree, then hit the sack." Bubba stood on his hind legs and begged to be picked up. Howard tapped his chest, and the dog jumped into his arms. I watched as they casually walked over to a cusp of oak.

Mason came later, still damp from his dip in the tank. "You gonna tell me where we are headed? I may not want to keep heading west."

"Well, I've been thinking about it and have decided that Lacy and I want to go home. Montana, southwest corner. Winter sounds

wonderful, and all that cold weather should affect the walkers. I'd understand if you want to go somewhere else, but that is where we're headed."
He thought on for a few moments, then said, "Always wanted to go to Montana. I love the mountains too. Sounds perfect to me. Thanks for inviting me along. I appreciate it."
I nodded, secretly pleased he wanted to come along. I don't know what it meant, being so happy about it, but I wasn't going to give it much more thought. I just nodded at him and finished up the kitchen cleanup.
Lacy and I got the big bed, so she helped Mason make the bunk up for him. He had wanted to sleep in the truck, but the RV had solar panels, and we would be able to run the air all night since I had picked up the biggest batteries I could find. I think that was the deciding factor for him. Lights went out in the four outfits slowly, and we were left with just crickets for background noise. I thought it sure beat motorcycles and car alarms as I started to relax.
Then I went to sleep in a flash and didn't dream a thing that night.

CHAPTER 3

We were in New Mexico a little after 1 o'clock the next day. After a brief lunch and done lengthy discussion, we decided to start heading north as soon as possible. There were oral Wells everywhere, making you wonder why we used to import oil. The scenery change from bass, rose-colored deserts to Broken maces and high snow-capped peaks on the mountains in the distance. We saw numerous cacti and yucca, which kept Lacy busy looking up plants in her New Mexico travel guide she had checked out of the Texas library. There were wild turkeys, porcupines, deer, and an abundance of other wildlife. I knew there were rattlesnakes around. New Mexico had adopted the black bear as their state animal, so although I hadn't seen any, I hoped we could avoid them. The temperature hadn't improved, and the heat was beginning to get to the vehicles. Duke's bus decided to act up just south of Albuquerque, so we stopped under a small grove of trees while Howard checked it out. We were on a gravel road to bypass Albuquerque. We were on a gravel road, although there wasn't much gravel, and we hadn't seen any walkers for a while, which was a welcome relief, but the dust was horrible. We decided to have a small siesta while we rested, so Mason agreed to go hunting. While I entertained thoughts of a roasted turkey, Sarah and Mandy dozed in the shade of a pinon pine.

Soon, I saw Howard and Duke walking toward us, frowning, and I knew the news wasn't good.

"Well, near as I can tell, it's all this blasted dust that's clogged up the air filter, and I would imagine if I looked at all the outfits, they would need their filters cleaned. I have some new ones, but the ones we need to be blown out, so I'd rather do that than replace them. The heat isn't helping either. I need to change the thermostat on the bus."

Mason came around the RV with a turkey slung over one shoulder. I know my eyebrows climbed up into my bangs, bringing a smile to his face.

"There's a farmstead about two miles down the road." He said.

"It has the biggest barn I've ever seen and several pole barns. But before you get too excited, I think you should turn around and look toward the west.

We have a nasty-looking storm headed this way, and I sure would like to be out of the weather before it hits."

We all turned toward the area, like we were all tied to the same string, and saw a black nasty wall cloud rolling towards us.

"Howard, can the bus make it two miles?" I asked

"Far as I'm concerned." He and Duke hurried over to the bus, and everyone scurried to their rides, with Mason leading the way again. When we arrived at the farmstead, I was impressed. It was one of those Mexican haciendas painted a rose color with rounded roof corners and wood beams sticking out along the bottom of the roof. It lacked several clumps of red chili hanging from the rafters. In the rear was an enormous barn. I'd seen more pole buildings than an average person could ever use.

When I pulled up, Mason had already opened the barn door and disconnected his trailer. He pulled into the opposite door, got out, and opened the door so that I could pull inside. I got as close to his bumper as I could. He had pulled the trailer under the smaller pole barns, then ran back and closed the massive barn door.

I parked and ran outside to ensure the bus and

wrecker were safely in the pole barns, although the rear of the wrecker stuck out a bit. Howard just shrugged and came out with the rest of us to watch the approaching storm.

There is something almost mystical about a thunderstorm. It's scary, exhilarating, and humbling. You could feel the electricity in the air making the tiny hairs on your arm stand up and smell the rain in the air. Mother nature is a rough taskmaster, and she lets you know on the occasion that there is something in life more significant than you. The storm rumbled toward us, and we retreated into the barn to wait it out when it was near.

The rain was dumped on us by the truckloads. Hail followed in intervals on the tin roof, sounding like a machine gun going off. The thunder sounded like volleys of canons repeatedly firing in the distance, and lightning zipped across the sky, blinding us. The temperature plummeted compared to earlier.

    The wind pushed the rain almost horizontally in intensity, scaring the hell out of everyone. Mandy ran to Duke, crying, as the noise continued for half an hour, then it tapered off and ended. Bubba was jumping up on Mandy, trying to get her attention. When he did, he let her chase him around the barn. It was dark out, but I realized it was late in the day, and we were looking at dusk. We left the rear door of the barn open, letting in the clean air and slight breeze.

"I think we have a problem," Duke said. We all turned toward him and saw him looking out of the barn through a crack in the wall. Mason and I made our way to the wall and peeked out a gap in the boards. Two Humvees were parked behind the house and must have come in during the storm. I returned to the RV, retrieved a walkie-talkie, and turned the sound on low.

"Yes, sir... we're sitting out the worst of it." static, then "We'll be heading out in about five minutes." We looked at each other, then motioned to Sarah to retrieve Mandy while Duke slipped out the back of the barn. He'd be busy spreading the new tarps over the wrecker and bus.

We continued to hear static, but the men in the Humvee remained quiet. After several minutes, one man got out and went to the back of the house to relieve himself, then returned to the Humvee, and both vehicles pulled out and went back the way we had come. "Sir, we went to the next town and saw nothing. All clear." We listened a while longer but didn't hear anything of value. We decided to keep the walkie on and have someone monitor it.

Howard and Duke had been working on the bus and checking the filters in all the vehicles. We were trying to decide when to leave, knowing we needed to put some distance between them and us. There was no telling if they would return or not, and we didn't want to be here if they did.

We discussed it a lot when I noticed something odd about the house. I couldn't put my finger on what was bothering me. I motioned to Mason, and he wandered over from the truck. "What's up?" he asked as he cleaned dirt and grease from his hands on a rag.

"That house does seem strange to you, and before you say anything, please just look at it a moment." He had opened his mouth to say something, then closed it and turned to study the house. I was glad to see him look at it cause most people would've argued with me. Then he tilted his head a bit, leaned forward, and looked at it.

"Grab your bow," he said, then turned and went to his truck. I geared up and grabbed my night vision goggles, found Lacy, and explained what we were doing. She wasn't happy but promised to watch things. "How do I get that turkey into the oven? It's huge."

"Don't mess with it right now or until we get back. We won't be long. If we have to, we'll cut it up a bit." She seemed okay with that idea and went back to flipping through a magazine. I'd have thought she had read them several times by now. Mason and I crept up to the side of the house, peering into every window we came to. A flash of light from the front of the house gave us a start, and we froze. Luckily I was next to an electrical meter, and that's when I finally realized where the low humming sound I was hearing was coming from. Tapping Mason on the arm, I pointed at the meter, and then we both leaned towards it and stared closely at it until we saw the little wheel turning at the bottom. We looked at each other simultaneously, smacking the goggles and pulling a squeak from me before we jumped back. I needed to chill out. My nerves were a mess. Mason slowly walked around the house and stood in front of the picture window. When I got there, I did the same thing, watching the snowy static on the TV set. Yee haw! I tapped Mason on the arm excitedly. He tilted his head at me. I whispered, "electric water heater, electric stove, electric freezer...ice cream, ice, pizza, blah, blah, blah." and danced a bit in place to emphasize my excitement. He straightened up and looked back and forth from me to the TV and back. About then, the damned walker stumbled into the front room. I tilted my head back and forth slowly and thought, "some things are worth working for but damn, come on."

We headed back to the barn, both quiet but eagerly anticipating all the many wonders electricity provided. When we arrived in the RV, everyone looked at us, waiting. "Well," I said, "The house has electricity." Everyone started to talk at the same time. "Wait a minute...we have to finish the work on the outfits, and while that is happening, I think we should, at the very least, find out if there is a freezer in there."

"Oh hell yeah," Lacy said excitedly. "I'll help you." Mason cleared his throat and said, "I think we need you here, so when we're ready, we can leave."

"But I thought we were at the very least staying the night. Why do we have to leave so soon?"

"The Humvees that were here earlier? We don't want them to come back and find us here. We must get the outfit's road ready, check the house, and leave around midnight. Is that okay with everyone? We can stop somewhere tomorrow morning and sleep before going on."

"But why do we have to avoid the military? They are supposed to be our friends?" Sarah asked.

"Well, they are supposed to be our friends, but we don't know for sure, and there is no way to find out without letting them know about us. We are better off assuming they aren't friendly than taking the chance they are. We don't need them right now anyway."

"We need some more fuel, too. We're all low, and 'though I plan to use the backup gas cans, we will need to replace them as soon as possible."

"I agree, Howard. So let's plan on leaving at midnight, and can everyone be ready by then?"

When everyone, including Mandy, Mason, and I, returned to the house.

We planned to make some noise entering the house. Walkers are attracted to noise, which beats sneaking around and getting surprised by one. That almost happened anyway. The walker in the front room came barreling right at me, but Mason nailed him in the top of the head with a huge knife. We'd come in the back door, stomping and slamming the door, then swept through each room like police officers. Yelling "Clear" and going high and low as we saw on TV shows as we made our way back to the front room. Mason turned off the TV and unplugged the clocks and microwave, so no lights were visible within the house. I met him back in the kitchen, and we grinned like kids. He did the old stumble back and two-step when he opened the pantry. I don't know how it got in there, but a naked female walker had gotten herself locked in the pantry until he opened the door. I don't think I could have stumbled about so wildly and kept my feet, so I was impressed when he did. I pulled up the bow and planted an arrow in its left eye. I grabbed it by its foot and gave Mason a look that encouraged him to hold the other foot. I'm good at giving looks. It takes years of hard work and dedication, but you must be good at something.

We dragged it into the front room out of the way, then went back to the kitchen. I figured anything in the fridge would be a chemist's delight, with the green fuzzies, so I just went to the freezer. Bingo! Yep, I knew there had to be ice cream in there...one of those big two-gallon tubs with a handy dandy carrying handle looked new, well, not opened anyway. There were packages of hamburgers, steaks, pizza, and butter. I knew we couldn't take it all, we didn't have one freezer among us, but I couldn't help myself.

I went to the bedroom and found several plastic totes filled with clothes and blankets on the closet floor. Dumping the contents on the floor, I took the totes back to the kitchen and began to load food in them. Mason watched with a smile, and when one was complete, he put the lid on it and began to drag it to the back door. I stopped him, held up one finger, and thought to Lacy, *"Sis, would you ask Howard and Duke to come to the back door?"*

"Sure, is everything okay?"

"Yep."

I then told Mason to watch for the boys while I searched the area for other things we might be able to use. He thought back. *I didn't know you could do that, and it might come in handy in the future. Is Lacy the only one you talk to that way?*

"Yep, don't tell the others, though, they might feel uncomfortable being around us, and I don't want that." He gave me the thumbs up and went to the door when the boys arrived to help carry the heavy totes back to the barn. After filling the oven with three pizzas, I continued my search and stumbled onto fudge, caramel, strawberry sauce, coconut, and peanuts. Yep, I was thinking the same thing. Banana Splits, here we come.

We ended up with three totes of food. Carrying three pizzas and silverware, I hurried back to the RV. My mouth had been watering as the smell of the pizza filled the house, and I couldn't wait to sink my teeth into one.

The party was in full swing when all of a sudden, I got an uneasy feeling. I held a hand up, and everyone instantly quieted. I listened but couldn't hear anything. It was then that Bubba went into a crouch and growled low, his hackles standing straight up. I grabbed my bow, and while Lacy turned out the lights, Mason, Howard, and Duke followed me."What is it?" Howard whispered.

"I'm not sure, but there is something out there. It's too quiet. We need someone in the loft," I whispered.

Duke went to the loft while the rest tried to see outside. Mason started to say something else to me, but I put my hand across his mouth. I moved my head from side to side, trying to get the best reception; that's the best way I can explain it. There were soldiers in the house. I felt like they weren't supposed to be here as I kept getting thoughts of apprehension and haste. I couldn't identify any specific thoughts as we were too far away.

Howard locked the barn doors. He covered the wrecker and bus earlier, so I wasn't worried about them. We watched as their flashlight beams moved from one room to the other. A lot of time was spent in the bedrooms when it finally dawned on me they were stealing jewelry.

The back door of the house opened, and I tensed. Mason began to screw the silencer onto the end of his rifle while I armed my bow. We waited, ready, while the man approached the barn. Then the other guy said, "I must be going crazy," one whispered to the other, "I smell pizza." The other guy tapped him on the shoulder and said, "come on, we're wasting time." The soldier headed towards us hesitated a moment, then they both turned back towards the house. Soon, we heard the sound of a truck and watched as they went back down the road.

"Let's get out of here. I can't take much more tonight," I said as Mason leaned against the door. He looked at me, grabbed me behind the head, and pulled me to him. The kiss was long and hard and satisfying. While I was learning to breathe again, he muttered something and walked back to his truck.

"Well." I thought as I watched his fine backside disappear into the dark. I shook my head and went back to the RV to tell Lacy to batten down the hatches. We were leaving in half an hour. We left with lights out and tail lights covered. Using the night goggles, we drove another four hours that night.

Criss-crossing the interstate when we found the road blocked by pileups took its toll on our nerves. Exhausted and cranky, we finally found a ball field on the outskirts of a small town and parked behind the tall bleachers. I was concerned I would be too tense to go to sleep, but exhaustion finally won out, and I fell asleep to the sound of owls in the distance and a cool breeze from the north. I dreamed of Montana that night, making me more determined than ever to return.

CHAPTER 4

The smell of coffee dragged me out of bed. I pulled on my jeans and tee shirt and stumbled into the kitchen. It was full. I stopped in my tracks and felt my eyebrows raise. Lacy turned towards the counter and handed me a mug of coffee. I took a sip, sighed then eyed the group.
"What's up?" I asked and sat at the table. We were having pancakes this morning as a platter was heaped high in the middle of the table, and syrup of different flavors was lined up nearby.
I smiled at Mandy, who had syrup on her nose, and the biggest smile radiating from her face. She did love to eat. Bubba even got in on the fun as he had his plate of cakes and was busy chowing down.
"We were going to ask if there was any way we could take a few days off. We're all a little wiped out, and it's been a crazy few days, and our butts are dragging." Howard said as he washed his plate.

"Mine is too. I had planned to rest up for a couple of days when we got to Moab, Utah. That's where the Arches National Park is, and I've been there. It's beautiful and quiet and has shade trees. I thought it would be a wonderful place to chill out for a few days. The weather will still be hot but drier."

Everyone looked at each and nodded.

Mason wiped his mouth and said, "I think we can wait a bit longer. We have some fuel, but we will have to stop soon. I looked at the map and saw a truck stop a few miles down the road in Utah, and I think it might be a good place to get fuel."

"OK, let's plan to leave in half an hour?" Lacy put a plate in front of me, and I put two pancakes on it. While I ate, everyone went out to get their outfits ready to go.

It was a beautiful, clear day, and you could see for miles. In the distance was "Shiprock Formation." A rock formation over 1500 feet high and sacred to the Navajo Indians. The sky above it was the prettiest blue in sharp contrast to the sands of the high desert. It was still early, but the temps were in the mid 80's at least. I was getting antsy to head north.

We headed west, leaving New Mexico behind.

Clipping the northeast corner of Arizona, we soon arrived in Utah. The breathtaking canyons and majestic mountains we had just gotten used to seeing turned into narrow, chaotic canyons and steep, confining barrier reefs. Then we once again traversed land that was broad, open, and windswept. We continued north and were almost to Blanding when we encountered a hitchhiker. Hitchhikers were new to us, so we were wary. Mason was driving the truck instead of his bike because of the heat and said he would check things out while we headed up the highway. I wondered when we decided to let Mason lead the way. No one had seemed upset by it, and I wasn't either, but it did make me wonder. I'm not one to relinquish control like that, but then I reasoned that if I was kept in the loop, I didn't have a problem with it. I made a note to myself that I would discuss it with the rest of the group to see what their feelings were.

Mason said he was picking up the man, and we should meet at the truck stop about 22 miles ahead. Since the stranger was riding with Mason, I figured it was OK, but I wanted to meet the guy before we spent the night with him.

We pulled into the truck stop and parked next to a

fuel truck. I looked around for Howard and motioned him over while Mason talked to the hitchhiker. "Is there any easy way to get the fuel from this truck instead of getting it from the pumps or siphoning it from cars?"

He walked over to the truck, then climbed inside. After fiddling around in the cab for a few minutes, he started the big rig up, sending clouds of black smoke billowing in the air overhead. He climbed back down and walked to the back of the tank, where after looking around, he motioned me over. "We can hook up a hose to this valve, open a valve on top, and gravity will force the fuel out of the tank. Just pull up next to me, and I'll fill you up. I'll get the bolt cutters out to cut the padlock on the hose while you're doing that." He said and walked back to the wrecker. He talked to Duke on the way, who began to move the big bus into position behind me.

It didn't take long to fill the rigs and the empty gas cans in the back of the bus. I'd let Bubba out of the wrecker to find a tree and noticed Mason walking the stranger back to me. The guy wasn't much to look at. Tall, skinny, dirty, and sunburned as severely as I've seen anyone. He carried a backpack, which had a folding fishing chair attached to it and a guitar, and he held a hunting rifle.

"This is Randy," Mason said. "He's looking to hook up with someone that can take him to Seattle cause he heard there was a refugee center there, and I told him I've never heard of it."

"I heard it on the radio before I left Denver, and everyone was headed there." He whined when he talked, and I HATE whiners! I looked at Mason, and he just shrugged.

"Not everyone, Randy. There was a rumor in Florida that a refugee center was in Denver, and since then, I've read half a dozen fliers saying there were more. There aren't any refugee centers, and they've all been overrun. We are alone out here and have to fend for ourselves."

He looked from me to Mason and back again. "Can I go with you then?" he whined. I cringed.

"Why are you walking?" I asked curiously.

"I can't drive. I know how," he said quickly, looking at his feet. "It's just that I got into a fight with a walker, broke my glasses, and now I can't see to drive. I tried once but ran into a bridge railing and almost fell into the river. I can't swim either."

"Of course not," I said quickly and got a look

from Mason.

"What?" I asked him.

Shaking his head, he turned to Randy. "In our group, everyone has a say. While we explore, they can discuss it, and we'll know when we get back." He said, "We're going shopping. Would you ask Duke to bring his heat detector with him? I want to clear the truck stop before we go in."

Nodding my head, I talked to Duke and moved the RV into a shade. One of just two such places in the whole country as far as I could see. Going inside, I saw Lacy looking out the window and asked: "Who's the new guy?"

"He isn't new till we talk about it. I have a good feeling about him, but I'm not sure what the deal is yet."

"Did you use your mojo?" she said as she popped the top on the soda.

"Not yet. I wasn't able to get past the whine. I'm hoping Mason will, and I don't want to dig around in his head from how he looks outside."

"Yeah, I get that. You'd think he could have found a puddle somewhere to clean up. I could smell him from the inside of the RV."

Shots could be heard from inside the truck stop. We jumped out of the RV and started to run

toward them when Howard stopped us.
"Give them a minute before you run in blind."
Soon Duke, Mason, and Randy emerged from the truck stop. Randy and Mason carried a couple of bags, and I could hear Randy's excited voice. When he looked up, he wore a new pair of reading glasses.
"There were walkers inside. Got Randy here some glasses and new clothes. Would you mind if he showered in the RV? He ain't getting back in my truck till he smells better." He looked at Randy and said, "Sorry about that, buddy, but you are foul." Randy grinned and nodded. "It would be mighty nice of you, ma'am. My mama didn't raise me this way, and I hate to offend anyone, but I ain't good on my own."
"As long you never call me ma'am again." I nodded my head, and he headed to the RV. Lacy jumped out to avoid him, and I looked at Mason. He got the point and followed him to show him how the shower worked. I had no idea where he was going to sleep till I noticed Howard strolled out of the truck stop with a large, black container. I found out it was a tent you set up on the top of your vehicle. It even had a latter. I smiled big at that, and grinning, Howard shook his head and

climbed into the wrecker. He started feeding something to Bubba, and I knew he had found some treats.

We sat at the table talking about Randy when the shower shut off. Lacy had fixed a fruit platter, and we worked on it when Randy came out of the bathroom. I knew my mouth fell open at the transformation. He looked around 18 years old, tall with sandy hair that needed cutting. His new clothes were too big but significantly improved over his dirty ones. "Just throw the old clothes away in the dumpster. We have no way to wash them, and I would guess they would be impossible to get clean anyway."

Lacy glanced in his direction when he walked past the table, and her mouth fell open. "Wow," she muttered. "Is that the same guy? Wow." We all smiled at her.

"Have you noticed we have been climbing in elevation? It is just over 4,000 feet at Moab, so it should be cooler, but I won't promise anything. We'll stay at the Arches National Park for a couple of days before going to Montana."

"How much longer before we reach Montana?" asked Sarah. "I'm ready to settle down."

"Let's see, probably about two more days on the

road, I hope."

Randy knocked on the door, and Lacy nearly knocked Duke down getting to the door. Duke yelled, "Come in," and grinned real big when Lace scowled at him.

Randy came in and stood looking down at his feet. I looked down to see what the fascination was and saw new Nike's on huge feet.

"Here, you can have my seat," Lacy said. "I'll get you a soda. Help yourself to the fruit. Oh dear, I bet you're starving. How about I fry you some Spam?" Lacy was moving back and forth from the fridge to the table, and people were scrambling to get out of her way. Even Bubba was managing to keep from being stepped on. He finally went to the back and lay down on the bed, watching the proceedings with big brown eyes.

Lacy noticed that Randy had cleaned up pretty well. I knew I was in for an exciting time of it now. You could tell he wasn't used to all the attention and was turning redder by the minute. Without

a word, we all went outside. "The way I figured it, another hour will get us to Moab and the Arches, so when Randy is settled, we can leave. Mason, can you drive the fuel truck?"

He turned and studied the truck, then smiled at me. "I like the way you think. How full is it?" He asked Howard as I wandered over to Sarah.
"You two holding up, OK?
"Yep, just tired like everyone else." Mandy was playing with Bubba. She would toss the ball, and Bubba would take after it, ears flopping and tongue hanging out."I'll be glad to have a kitchen, bathroom, and soft bed."
"Amen to that." Just then, Randy and Lacy joined the group.
"Mason is gonna drive the fuel truck, so Lacy, you OK to drive his truck?"
"Sure, can Randy ride with me?" I looked at Randy, smiled nicely, and said, "You know she is my sister, right," He blushed as Lacey moaned, "J.D."
"Yes, ma'am, and I promise to behave myself."
"Good, I shoot first, ask questions later."
"OK," he mumbled.
Everyone went to their outfits and climbed inside before we proceeded north. As we neared Moab, the right side of the road consisted of housing developments that sported large, square areas of green grass, startling against the desert backdrop. On the left side were high, jagged, rusty-colored

cliffs jutting towards the sky. The closer to town we got, the more civilization opened up on both sides of the road, and we began to see walkers on the side streets. Rock formations reaching to the sky, every color of the rainbow, weathered and jagged, took your breath away.

Mason pulled the huge fuel truck ahead and sped up a bit. Soon I noticed walkers being propelled out on either side of him and knew he was clearing the road. I hated doing it that way, it was just plain gross, but I also knew we had no choice. Another half hour and we arrived at the park site. We parked and started to unload chairs, unwind the awning on the RV, and set up umbrellas for the bus.

We milled about, stretching and moaning. The sound of Masons' radio vibrated the ground as Lacy pulled into the lot next to us. As I approached the truck, the music abruptly stopped. The doors were swung open, and long-legged teenagers stepped to the ground. "I know, no noise, won't happen again, I promise," Lacy whined. Oh, no, I thought it was contagious. We walked back to the group, and I thought of where this would go, and I didn't want to go there.

"OK, some rules," I said. "No one wonders off

alone or enters a building or vehicle alone. At least two people together and carry walkies and weapons. Also, drink a lot of water and keep the noise level down. I want the showers and restrooms cleared right away and kept locked with the padlocks Duke will hand out. That way, they stayed clear. Does anyone want to add anything?" When no one said anything, I motioned to Sarah, and we began to prepare lunch after I got the two pullouts on the RV figured out.

I sat at the table and pulled the road map to figure out the trip's next leg.

"Can't that wait" asked Sarah as she fiddled at the stove ?"You've got two days to mess with that stuff, just relax, enjoy this incredible view and worry about that sister of yours."

I smiled at that and put the map away. Accepting a bottle of raspberry-flavored tea, I sat on the couch and sighed. I was about to fall asleep when a horrifying scream broke the silence, and the bottle hit the floor.

CHAPTER 5

I flew out the RV door and missed the bottom step. Since I had grabbed my crossbow as I exited, I landed on my stomach, and my bow slid across the gravel. Unfortunately, so did I. Ignoring the pain, which wasn't easy, I grabbed the damned bow again and took off in the direction everyone else was running, gravel flying from under my feet. The screaming continued, which was good if you thought about it long enough.

We were all running in the direction of the restrooms. The screaming was coming from the women's restrooms, and nearly all of us hit the door simultaneously. "Oh, for heaven's sake," I muttered, my heart about to beat out of my chest. Mason made it in first, and immediately a loud shot rang out, reverberating off the concrete walls of the restroom and inside my head. We all filtered inside and glanced down at the walker. , Then we looked up and found Lacy, standing on the top of the stalls, with her hands holding onto the pipes that ran across the ceiling into the men's section. The walker lay inside the first stall where Lacy stood. Please," she said shakily, tears sliding down her cheeks. Randy pushed his way inside and stood on the toilet, reaching up to take her hands, and eventually, she was down and crying on Randy's shoulder. Howard and Mason disposed of the walker, got out one of Duke's padlocks, and locked the door, placing the key on top of the drinking fountain near the entrance. It might seem odd to put it in plain sight, but walkers don't use keys; if it doesn't open, they go away.

"Lacy has to start paying attention, JD. She goes willy-nilly into space and doesn't think. Duke said, and I nodded at him because I thought the same thing. She's a teenager and doesn't think, and it almost got her killed again.

"I'll talk to her again, Duke, because I don't know what else to do. I can't force her to use good judgment when she is unfamiliar with it."

"Well, til then, you better let Sarah tend to those scrapes. Man, it looks like they should hurt." shaking his head, he wandered off to clear the men's room so he could padlock that door too.

As soon as he said the words, I hurt, yep, knees pulled like they would split wide open, and my back, Geesh! I refused to hobble but standing upright hurt. The palms of my hands were scraped and bleeding, and my elbows too. Great!

I hobbled into the RV, as any self-respecting walker-fighter from Montana would do. I had no shame, and when Sarah poured peroxide on my many wounds, I cried cause that's what you're supposed to do when someone puts acid on an open injury. I mean peroxide on open, deep wound-type scrapes. Right?

After I had relearned to breathe and wiped the tears away, I got a nice, new, cool bottle of raspberry tea and a pillow for my head on the lovely soft couch. I waited for the pain pill to take effect while I waited for Lacy. The pain pill made me nice and mellow, which is why she waited so long to come inside. I guess she thought I wouldn't yell, and she was right. Trying to think was painful, but I needed to deal with Lacy.

"Sis," she said quietly as she sneaked inside, "I'm real, sorry." (I heard that one before.) "I know we are supposed to clear the rooms first, but I really had to go bad, and well, anyway, no one got hurt."

I peeked out from under the cool cloth on my face.

"Well, you did, and I'm sorry, but it turned out almost OK. Please, don't be mad at me."

I struggled to sit up because I thought what I had to say would sound better if I were upright, but the little moaning noises I was making ruined the effect, so I just sighed instead. A noise from the doorway made me look, and a sad-looking Randy was poised to come inside, so I forcefully said "NO!" and he backed out and shut the door. "You could've been killed or worse, bitten." I put up my hand to silence her before she could whine. "We've been in this situation several times, and you still haven't learned. I realize you're only 16, and I should probably give you some leeway, but these are hard times..." Damn lost my train of thought. Think, think, think. Good drugs, what? Oh yeah. "You have seen these things in action, nearly been eaten alive by them on more occasions than I want to think, and still you do what you want. If you can't think of yourself, it's about time you thought of others. One of these days, we won't get there in time, and Lacy, I'm not going to be too keen on having to put a bullet in your brain and bury you. Shape up or ship out. That's all there is to say. Do you understand? The whole group is affected by what you do or don't do. You have to understand what your actions do to others."

By the time I had finished, she was in tears, and the drug effects were wearing off. I lay there waiting to see if anything I managed to say got past the hormones. I had done everything I could for her. She had to wake up and take responsibility even at her age, and she just had to. I let her cry herself out.

"I know what you say is true. I know you can't be there every time I screw up, and I would die if anything happened to you because of me. I promise I'll think about my actions more and try to learn from them. I'm going out now to apologize to everyone and promise them the same thing. I love you, sis, and I know you love me too. I'm sorry you got hurt. Rest, and I'll be back later to check on you." She kissed me on my chin, a spot I had somehow neglected to drag through the gravel, and left the RV, quietly shutting the door behind her. I didn't remember much until the smell of cooking roused me.

It took me several attempts to try to sit up. Muscles had tightened up, and my body had been switched with some old lady's while I slept. By the time I was upright, I was almost in tears again and panting like a dog in August. If I hadn't been so hungry, I would've just laid there and died, but nature was demanding an audience, so the direction I needed to go was up. I could hear voices outside the door, so I peeked out the window over the sink and saw the guys milling around the table. I turned and headed for the bathroom just as my bladder demanded. I took tiny steps across the floor, which suddenly seemed as vast and empty as the desert. I covered it inch by painful inch. I had a lot of time to watch my feet as I made my way the ten feet to the bathroom. When I completed my journey, I turned and shuffled back to the kitchen, stepped down two steps: ow, stood on the gravel, and thanked the gods. Everyone was watching me. Mason couldn't decide whether he should help me or not and was worried about it till I shook my head at him. He still wavered between sitting and standing as I made my painfully slow progress to the picnic bench.

Everyone sighed along with me when I finally settled at the table. I smiled at everyone while they tried not to look at my wounds.

"Hi," I said and smiled, "What's for dinner?"

Everyone started talking at once. The guys had secured the area, and the body was gone. Some of the group wanted to go hiking on some trails after dinner, and they agreed. I guess Lacy wanted to take pictures of the rock formations, and Randy just wanted to stare at her. I would not be going as someone needed to stay with the camp, and I elected to do it. Howard said he needed to check the vehicles out, and Bubba needed a nap so that he would stay behind too.

Sarah and Lacy finished dinner, and we sat down to eat. I drank a lot of water and later discovered that the pain meds had made me thirsty. I waited till they left for their hike before slowly making my way back to the RV and the couch. Sarah followed me inside, got me a couple of aspirin, then sat at the table and fiddled with some papers.

"What's up, Sarah?" She looked miserable.

"I was wondering what Montana was like." I knew that wasn't what was bothering her, and I knew she would get around to it eventually, so I described snow-capped mountains that caressed the endless sky, air so crisp and cool you could take a bite out of it and the sky at night so filled with stars it brought tears to your eyes. When I finished, she still looked miserable.

"Spit it out, Sarah."

"I think I'm pregnant. I haven't said anything to Duke yet, cause I'm not 100 percent sure, but I have a pretty good idea. I don't know what to do, and I don't want to raise a child in a world as crazy as this one."

"Let's wait and get a pregnancy test, and when we know for sure, we'll go from there. Whatever happens, we will figure it out. Just let me pick up one of those tests the next time I can, and we will find out for sure. OK? We will do this. I'll be there for you no matter what you decide to do."

She looked at the tiny pieces of paper she had shredded on the table, and a tear slowly slid down her pretty face. She nodded, then went outside, stopping at the door. "Thanks, JD. I won't tell Duke till we know for sure. Get some rest." Then she closed the door, and I stared at the ceiling for a long time.

I thought I had problems.

The following day brought with it a lot of boredom. You could tell that everyone had had their fill of the rugged scenery and was borderline antsy. I was still sore as hell, but I offhandedly mentioned leaving like a day early, and everyone just started taking down awnings and putting up folding chairs. Lacy helped me with the pull-outs, and awning as I was moving snail slow, and SHE said I was making little pain noises. Mason pulled

the fuel truck out into the middle of the lot, and we took turns fueling up. While I waited for the others to fuel, I got out the map and lined up our route. I looked up to see Mason at my window. "The fuel truck is nearly empty, so I'm going to leave it and drive the pickup truck until we find another one. Randy is going to ride with me, and we're all ready to go anytime you are."
"Let's go then, "I said and put the RV in gear. We drove from rugged, barren, jagged
cliffs to multi-colored rock formations and high mountain passes covered with Douglas fir, lodge pole, and yellow pine. Willow and cottonwoods lined the river that crisscrossed under the highway a dozen times. Douglas Pass sits at an elevation of over 8000 feet, and at the top is a road garage and weather station. The road snaked around the mountains, and the going was slow and hard on the nerves.
A few miles down the road, we came to a small town, and on the main street, there was a small pharmacy. I radioed that I needed to stop at the pharmacy, and the caravan stopped in front of the store. Mason and I approached the store while Duke took the top of the bus, and Lacy and Randy stood guard on the sidewalk.

"What are you looking to find? Maybe I can help." Mason whispered.
"I think I could probably find it faster myself. It's in the feminine hygiene section." He blushed a bit and walked to the back of the store. I grabbed a sack and located several pregnancy tests, after-morning pills, condoms, and prenatal vitamins. As an afterthought, I grabbed tampons and anything else to throw in the sack to cover the other items. That was what I had in hand when Mason returned. "We need to leave." I started to the front of the store when shots were fired outside.
Shit, that's all we needed. Mason grabbed the door, and as Duke slid off the bus, I slipped into the RV, and just by the skin of our teeth, we made it out of town. Lacy was driving while I watched that everyone else got left oK.
We started seeing wildlife which was a real treat after the barrenness we had seen. Antelope and deer seemed to be in abundance, but the land soon became barren again, with mountains in the distance that reached for the sky. I sincerely hoped we didn't have to drive over any more passes.
The sun reflected off the rock walls, and scrub brushes dotted the landscape. The road I had

chosen was miserable with switchbacks, tough inclines, steep downhills, and scary drop-offs. High cliff walls threw us into darkness, only to drop us again into the sun. It was similar to a roller coaster ride, and only you were the one steering, but no less scary. I found a rock road just outside Rock Springs, Wyoming, and we stopped for the night. We could barely walk, me doubly so with the scraped knees.

"If anyone else wants to figure out the routes, that is fine with me, but I can guarantee I will never drive through a mess like that again. The maps were deceiving and didn't show the roads clearly." When they just stood there and stared at me, I waved a hand at them, slowly and carefully made my way back into the RV, got out the bottle of gin, and made myself a drink. I deserved it, earned it, and dared anyone to stop me.

Lacy came inside and plopped down on the couch. "Well, at least it's cooler." she sighed. "I'm too nervous to eat, maybe just a pop tart." She watched me for a minute, got up, got the pastry, and went back outside after looking in my direction again. I made another drink.

Another 10 minutes brought everyone inside, and they just stared at me. I waved my hand toward the cabinets and said, "pop tarts." There was a snicker and then another, and the whole group laughed. I pointed at the gin bottle, saluted them with my glass, and started laughing also. That's what frayed nerves do to you, mass hysteria.

"We're leaving early, so take a Valium, eat a little something, and go to bed. Dream of flat land and green grass. Duke, what day is it?"

Duke thought a minute, frowned, then smiled big, "It's Friday. Why?"

"I plan to be at the end of the road for Sunday dinner. I can't promise we won't have any more crappy roads like today, but it will get better. Two days, folks."

There was head nodding and some people talking, then everyone filtered out to their beds. I watched Lacy and Randy eye each other, then kiss goodnight. I dreamed of falling off a mountain top onto a marshmallow.

Don't ask.

CHAPTER 6

I was up early the following day fixing coffee when Sarah came in. I looked outside, then bent and pulled the garbage can from under the sink, took out the trash bag, and pulled out the hidden pharmacy bag. Then replaced the can back under the sink.

"Go to the restroom," I said while preparing the coffee maker.

She didn't say a word, just went into the restroom and returned after a long time. I couldn't look at her. "Not pregnant," she said and sniffed.

"Are you sure? There were three tests in there."

"I used them all, and they all said the same thing." She sat at the table and fiddled with the road maps, and I took them away since she had shredded the Utah map the day before. I handed her a napkin, and she giggled.

"I think I'll talk to Duke and let him know how close we'd come. I saw the after-morning pills and

the condoms, and were they for me also?"
"Actually," I said as I sat across from her. "I was hoping Duke could talk to Randy and give the condoms to him. You know, in case he doesn't have his own."
Sarah raised her eyebrows at me and covered her mouth with her hand, stifling a laugh. "Oh, JD, you can't for one minute think that Randy's going to take advice from Duke or that Duke would even contemplate talking to him about sex with Lacy? Oh, my God, that is too funny.
"What's too funny?" asked Duke as he came in, Mandy not far behind.
Getting up to pour the coffee, Sarah looked at Mandy, then back at Duke, and just shook her head. Duke caught the look, smiled, sat at the table, and blew softly into his mug. Soon the RV was full of people, and I went into the back to clean up and change clothes. The smell of pancakes and fried spam filled the air, and I joined the festivities.
"You know, when we get settled, I don't want to see one pancake or smell even a little whiff of spam for a long time. Someone is going to go hunting and bring back an elk, and we're going to process it and have elk burgers and steaks, and

well, you know what I mean." I said as I sat down at the table. "A nice big elk roast, with potatoes and carrots and gravy, served with homemade bread....hm" Everyone sighed and then stared at the pancakes. Sighing, I speared one and poured blueberry syrup on top. Oh well.

We were soon back on the road and hadn't gone far when we spotted another fuel truck sitting at a truck stop, so Lacy and Randy got to drive Mason's truck again. The music was so loud the car bounced down the road, and I didn't care because Sarah wasn't expecting and we were almost home.

The land had turned flat with mountains on both sides, and we made good time. Large expanses of scrub brush dotted the ground and would magically disappear near the rivers, replaced with willows and cottonwoods so green it hurt your eyes. You could look at the flatland and come down a hill, and there would be a small town in front of you. Then you go up the mountain on the other side and look in your rearview mirror, and the city has disappeared special effects at their best. I thought I saw a deer in the distance, but when we got closer, I noticed it was a walker. Way out in the middle of nowhere, he was shuffling along in the scrub brush, with no particular place to go. When he caught sight of us, he became a little more energized, heading in our direction, but we soon lost sight of him.

Around midday, we pulled off the road into a wooded area near a small river. Bubba took off with Mandy close behind, and Lacy and Randy wandered off in their direction. Lacy kept an eye on Mandy so Sarah could help with the cooking. I think Lacy got the better end of the deal, but no one complained, so I didn't either. I was getting ready to call everyone to lunch when Mandy screamed. What the hell, I thought, and off we raced toward the river. I was getting tired of running toward the sounds of screams. We arrived to find Mandy on the ground crying and Randy beating on what looked like a rope near the river. "Rattlesnake," Lacy said, tears streaming down her face. "He got her on foot."

I had no idea what to do, but Mason put a tourniquet above her ankle, picked her up, and ran to the RV. I ran ahead to open the door yelling at Lacy to get the medical books. He laid her on the bed, whispering and propping her up with pillows. I sat near her and tried to talk to her, but Sarah nudged me out of the way. Soon she had Mandy nearly on her lap, whispering to her, wet cloth Duke handed her. Wiping Mandy's sweating brow, she looked at me like I could do something. Lacy brought the books and the snake bite kit. I shook my head at the snake bite kit as I had read several articles on the dangers of damaging the skin further with the kits. Like I said a lot of time reading in the library. So we cleaned and washed the bite area, then wrapped the whole foot up tight to above the ankle with an ace bandage. Sarah gave her a bottle of water and encouraged her to drink as much as possible. She gave her something for the pain.

Mason left the room, and I, and accepted the cool followed. "The bite is on the top of her foot, not deep muscle, so I don't think she got much venom. Keeping the ace bandage on will constrict the blood flowing to her heart, but the deep veins will allow blood to flow freely from the heart back to the foot." I just looked at him, and he shrugged. "We learned a lot in the navy. She should be okay, but we must closely watch her. Keep her foot elevated."

   I pointed my chin in the direction of the bedroom, "Go in there and tell them that. They need to hear it." Shoulders slumped, Mason slowly walked back to the room to talk to Duke and Sarah. I smiled because I knew they would be grateful, and Mason was embarrassed about gratitude. I turned, and Howard was seated on the couch with Bubba.

"She was protecting Bubba here. That little girl in there was trying to protect this crazy, snoopy old dog, and she got hurt. We feel bad about it too".

I sat near them and petted Bubba, looking at me with big, sad eyes. "She's going to be okay, Bud, so don't you or Howard worry about it. It would have killed you, and we would have been upset about that, especially Mandy."

Lacy and Randy came in, and we nibbled on what we could find and talked low until Duke came out. He was visibly shaken but accepted the pop I offered and smiled a bit. "She's asleep. Sarah will be stuck like glue to her till she's sure about her. Mason said if it had gotten her in the leg, it would have been worse. But she'll be okay".

He nodded, looked towards the bedroom, and let himself out. I watched as he walked over to a tree and leaned against it, and I had to look away.

Duke decided we should continue, so that's what we did. Sarah and Mandy were transferred to the bus so Duke could keep an eye on them, and we continued down the road. I shouted when I saw the "Welcome to Montana" sign. Finally, I was home.

Before we got to the interstate, we stopped and fueled up once again. When we saw the rest area, we decided to spend the night.

The next day would be a short one, and I was ready. Mandy was doing okay but still in pain and running a fever. Lacy fixed supper of canned stew, and we all sat around and watched the stars, unable to unwind and worried about Mandy. Duke lay on the picnic table seat, chewing on a toothpick. "Ya know that today is July 16th?" When no one said anything, he said, "July 16th is my birthday."

We all looked at each other and, with no other signal, began to sing "Happy Birthday" to him. He just smiled and continued watching the stars. We finished and went back to watching the stars also. I can't say we're a rowdy bunch, no sir, not us. Howard lay on the table next to us, petting Bubba, who had curled up nearby. "Tell us about this place we're going, JD."

"Well, it's a big, old, log-style lodge. It has a great room with a massive river rock fireplace, a big old western bar, and a game room. Upstairs, there are six bedrooms, suites, and a laundry room. In the basement are a game room and several bedrooms. It's all hand-hewn logs with a big wrap-around deck. It backs up to a hundred-foot high cliff wall with two caves used for storage. A spring feeds a little creek and a footbridge to cross over the stream to get to the caves. There are several outbuildings, a greenhouse, chickens, and a garden space, and they had several cows when I was here last. I hope they're still there, but I wouldn't count on it.

I'm excited about the lodge's wind generator, so it had electricity, so I'm keeping my fingers crossed it still works. We will be a day's drive from several large cities but far enough in the mountains to be isolated. That way, if we need anything, we have access to it.

Winter comes early in the mountains, so we need to get settled so we can get winterized. I don't know how much wood is cut, if we need it, or if the wind generator is still working. But it is a prominent place with several cabins for privacy, we can defend it if necessary, and it could be home. Tomorrow will tell, and I can't wait."

"Sounds wonderful," Randy said, cuddling Lacy

against his chest as they watched the sky. "I'm road weary and haven't been at it as long as the rest of you. Does anyone else notice that red glow to the east? It almost looks like a fire." We all looked, and sure enough, a forest fire was ongoing around Billings. There was nothing we could do. Since the virus, a forest fire would have to burn itself out.

We slowly drifted quietly off to our beds. Mason checked on Mandy, gave her some more Tylenol for the fever and pain then climbed into the fuel truck to go to bed. I left Lacy and Randy to spoon in the starlight and climbed into bed, knowing I would be too wound up to sleep. The next thing I knew, it was morning.

Mandy's fever was down the next day, and we headed west.

Soon we turned south into the mountains, leaving the paved road for gravel, weaving around the mountains for several miles before coming to the main gate made of logs. The sign read "Lion's Lodge."

We drove over the cattle guard and about another mile of winding around a large hill until finally, it was in front of us just as I had described it. I noticed right away that the wind generator was still. There were no vehicles in the large parking area out front, and the front door was standing wide open. Chickens free ranged, but there were no other signs of livestock.

Several bodies littered the yard, and some windows were broken out, but I still sat there sporting the biggest grins. Everyone just sat in their outfits, staring. I was so relieved I almost cried. I could've sat there for the rest of the day. Then three walkers walked around the corner of the lodge.

"Oh, for Pete's sake, don't these people have a home?"

I sighed, got up, took down my bow, cocked it, took a deep breath, and stepped out to clean the house.

CHAPTER 7

I nailed the first one in the mouth. Then Mason shot the second and third. We stood in the yard and waited since sound attracts em, and if any were in the house, they should be walking out about yep, WHOA! Big boy. Bang! I slowly crept up the steps, the bow ready, when another one stepped out of the broken window. TWANG! Arrow through the eye, bang! Bullet through the ear. We were on a roll. Where the hell were they all coming from?
By the time the smoke cleared, I was out of arrows, Mason was reloading his rifle, and we both were sweat-soaked. I was reminded of a song. ' Walkers to the left of me, walkers to the right; here I am, stuck in the middle with you.' Yep, I was pumped up. It must have been the spam.
I counted eleven but wouldn't relax until every inch had been searched. We did the old cop routine through the downstairs and then up the

stairs. No closet went unsearched, and no restroom or pantry wasn't examined. Around furniture, under beds, and behind shower curtains, all received a thorough look-see. Mason and Randy secured the basement. Then the outbuildings got a good going over, and only one walker was found locked in the barn's tack room. I have no idea how he got in there. By the time we hauled the bodies into a pile and set them on fire, it was nearing afternoon.

We padlocked every outbuilding, so we knew it was secure. Randy and Lacy then chased chickens till they were back in the pen, then secured it so they'd stay there. I gave them each a black marker and told them to mark every egg they found. While they stood and looked at each other, I explained that come morning, when they went looking for eggs for breakfast, the ones that didn't have a mark would be a fresh eggs. They walked away, mumbling to themselves.

Later, I heard it was like an Easter Egg Hunt. Only they got to scribble on the eggs. And they did too. Some had happy faces, vampire faces, clown faces, they went all out on the eggs, and since Randy is an artist, some looked too good to let a hen sit on them.

Sarah was heating a large canned ham in the RV while we did our hunt and destroy mission. She had instant potatoes, corn, and sliced tomatoes she had found growing in the garden. There was a peach cobbler for dessert, and she said it was a welcome-home dinner. We did her meal justice and then went to work securing the lodge. The door needed reinforcing, and the window boarded over until it could be replaced.

An office was to the right of the great room, and it had a small room off of it with a small bathroom. We decided that would be the perfect place to set up the computer equipment. Monitors would display views from the cameras mounted on each corner of the lodge, one on the main entrance and one on the wind generator.

Duke had a dozen cameras that did everything but the dishes and a remote-controlled toy helicopter with a camera mounted on its belly. Duke liked his toys.

To the left of the great room was a library with head mounts of every animal known to Montana. I don't see how anyone could relax with all those eyes staring at them, but Howard decided he wanted that room for some reason. It shared a bathroom with the room connected to it, which also looked like an office.

I chose a bedroom upstairs, which was connected to the one Lacy chose with a bathroom. I know what that girl can do to a bathroom, so I wasn't too happy. Mason found one he liked on the opposite side of the building, sharing his bath with Randy. That still left two bedrooms upstairs and several in the basement.

The kitchen was huge. Sarah and I stood in front of the walk-in freezer and stared at it. "I don't think I want to open that door. Can you imagine what it would smell like if everything inside were rotten? Sarah said quietly.

"I think we should wait till the electricity is fixed, let everything inside freeze up, and then open the door. It wouldn't smell as bad, would it?"

"I don't know," she said, looking from me back to the freezer, "and I don't want to find out either. Let's leave it alone, but then we must worry about the fridge." We dutifully turned and looked at the fridge. It might have directions taped to the front, 'In case of long-term disconnection...' but it just sat in its stainless steel finery. We looked at each other again, then turned and ooo'd and ahhhh'd over the six-burner stove with double ovens, a huge island, and granite countertops.

We nearly came unglued when we opened the pantry and discovered the many gallon cans of every fruit and vegetable known to man. The room was bigger than my first apartment back in Missouri, and the steel shelves held cases of biscuit starters, gravies, and dessert mixes. We were amazed at the amount of food. We found a closet full of every cleaner that had ever been made, not to mention rodent killers and a first aid station. Well, that made sense.

We had been poised to write down all the things we would need to get through the winter, but so far, we hadn't written down much except for the fridge and freezer. We did write down black spray paint (for the windows) because we only had one case left. Mason and Randy came in and announced they had found one cow and corralled it, then handed me their lists. It was a short one too.

"I'm amazed this place is so well stocked. It must have been restocked just before the virus. We need to feed the cow until we set up a place where it'll be safe. Duke is working on the wind generator and thought he might be able to get it working."

That was good news since it's one of the many

reasons I'd chosen the lodge. After supper, I suggested a meeting of the minds, and everyone returned to work.

Sarah and Lacy were breaking down a twin bed to put in Sarah and Duke's area near the computer room for Mandy. She had been resting on the couch in the great room. That way, everyone that walked by would talk to her for a minute or ask if she needed anything. Bubba was curled up by her side, sleeping. She looked better today. The swelling in her foot had gone down, and the fever was gone.

When I had the RV empty, I moved it next to the chicken coop. Soon, I noticed the bus and wrecker parked next to it, and I looked until I found the fuel truck and found it parked near the side of the building. Frowning, I started out the side door when I was blinded by the porch light and jumped like I had been shot.

My heart hammered in my chest as I struggled to breathe again. Then it blinked and went out...the light, not my heart. I looked towards the wind generator, but it was still.

Mason had found himself a gas generator. A giant honking monster of a generator that he had filled with fuel. I watched as he fiddled with it, and this time it stayed running. He wiped his hands on a rag, looked up at me, and smiled his heart-stopping smile as he walked over.

"We should be able to run this for a week, but I'm not sure what all it's running except the porch light. You might want to look around and check the rest of the lodge for lights and things that don't need to be on." I nodded at him and started to turn when he grabbed me and kissed the hell out of me again. Then he tapped me on the ass, turned, and walked away.

I'd think about that later and went inside to check for lights. It took me a while, and I found a curling iron, two TVs, a million lamps, and one washing machine. The little green light on the fridge came on, and I shuddered at the thought of what was in it. Still creeped out, I unplugged the microwave and every clock. The game room had several casino games that came on and scared the crap out of me, so they got unplugged also.

I hadn't seen Duke in a while, so I looked and found him in the basement, in a small room that held the 'stuff' for the wind generator. He was mumbling to himself and cussing, so I left him to it. He can't rush genius; if he got that thing running, he would be a genius. I tiptoed out and went back upstairs.

The door had been fixed, and the window boarded over. I checked the other entries and found Howard nailing boards over the last sliding glass door. We now had one door to worry about, and it had its padlock. We will be secure tonight. My bones hurt. I was so tired, and I knew everyone else was worn to the nubbin also.

Duke plodded in and found us sitting in the dining room. We had taken all the small tables and made a long dining table. A bowl of mixed fruit, a platter of fresh, sliced tomatoes, and a pan of biscuits sat on the table. We just stared at the food, too tired to make a move.

"I heard we were having a meeting," Duke said around a mouth full of tomatoes...not a pretty sight.

"We must figure out what we need to get through the winter. We have some time yet, but if we need another wind generator, we need to get it now. When the lodge was up and running, they supplemented their electricity with a wind generator, and now we have to use it for all our needs. So do we need another one or not?"

"Another one wouldn't hurt. That is a big freezer. We also need to figure out some kind of fence to put around the place to keep the walkers out. I was thinking, if we go to town and get what we need in 53-foot trailers, we can use the trailers, end to end, on their side as fences. That way, we could let the cow free range. Then we could also use the trailers for storage."

"Good idea, I like it. A wind generator will take up a few trailers, and we can pick up a new fridge too." I looked at Sarah, and she grinned real big. She wasn't too keen on cleaning out the fridge either. "There's a blackboard behind the welcome desk. If you think of something, just write it down there."

"It seems like we have things pretty well ship shape in here. Are there objections to sleeping here tonight? I know we got pretty comfortable in our rigs, but the queen-size bed has my name written all over it, so I am trying it out tonight." Everyone looked at Mason, then Howard. They just

shrugged their shoulders. "If we're staying here, we need to hit the sack soon. I don't want any lights on tonight, and Duke still doesn't have the cameras up until he gets the electricity going."

"I'm almost there. Those wind generators are tricky things, but I think I know the problem.

Tomorrow I should have it goin"

I said my goodnights and strolled out of the dining room into the great room. Standing in front of the fireplace, I wondered if I had chosen well and if my choice would keep us safe. Then I wandered up the stairs down the short hall and into my new bedroom. Someone had laid out my pj's, and I smiled as I picked them up and went into the bathroom.

I dragged my tired butt over to the queen size bed with the huge comforter, pulled back the covers, and slid under the sheets.

Oh my God, I thought this feels wonderful. Then I cried myself to sleep.

CHAPTER 8

The crow of a rooster intruded on my sleep. I lay there confused at the sound, then rolled onto my back and stared at the ceiling fan that was slowly turning above me. Is the ceiling fan turning? What the hell? Oh, yeah, I remember now and stretched while trying to ignore my bladder. I squinted at my watch, sat up in bed, blinked at the time, and peered closer at the dial. It was after 10 am. What the hell? I flipped the covers off, walked to the window, and lost my breath. The snowcapped mountains in the distance brought tears to my eyes. When the virus hit, I was in Florida keeping Lacy company while our parents were in Italy trying to revive their marriage. I didn't think I would ever get back to Montana and with so many friends.

I heard banging coming from the front of the building, so someone was up. I hurried and dressed, pulling on new jeans, a chambray shirt, and black Nikes. I rushed downstairs and found

Howard finishing up the bracket for Duke's camera.

"Mornin" he said around a mouth full of screws. "The door is fixed, and the window is as good as it's gonna be. There's breakfast on that is killer. We let ya sleep in, and you needed it."

"Oh, and you don't."

"Never could sleep in. My eyes open all by themselves. Bubba has trouble sleeping too, but I think it's cause he sleeps all day."

"I'll be in as soon as I finish this last bracket. They got the best coffee in the world stocked here, and I sure would like another cup."

I turned back and noticed Duke's room had tables lined up against the wall with monitors, computers, and things. I also saw two sets of legs sticking out among the wires, one with an ace bandage, and realized one set belonged to Mandy. That made me feel a whole lot better.

I followed wonderful smells into the dining room and the buffet table near the door. Sarah had been busy. Coffee and mugs were standing ready, and I helped myself. I nodded at Lacy and Randy, who sat near the window talking softly, and wandered into the kitchen and a pleasant surprise. Someone had gone out and collected a lot of eggs and none with marks on them.

"Great idea about the eggs," she said as she cleaned out a cabinet. "There's scrambled eggs on the buffet table along with toast. Help yourself. I ate hours ago and couldn't sleep just thinking about this wonderful kitchen. Go. Go," she shooed me out the door. I went straight to the scramble eggs and was tempted to eat them from the bowl, but I got a plate like an average person.

I was enjoying a full stomach and hot coffee when Duke came in with Mandy limping alongside him. She was helping him a lot, and I thought she was also learning a lot about computers cause that's the way Duke was. Mandy gave me the thumbs up and smiled, then went to sit with her dad. The clicking of nails on the hardwood floors signal Bubba with Howard close behind.

"Those brackets are ready when you are Duke."

"Thanks, Howard. I'll get to them in a minute. Mandy and I wanted more orange juice, isn't that right, Mandy girl?" Mandy gave the thumbs up again, and we all smiled. She had an orange mustache.

Everyone soon filtered out to do whatever. I was left standing there wondering what to do. When did I become idle? I asked myself as I went upstairs. I did some housekeeping and then wandered back to the kitchen. Mandy was sucking down some more orange juice at the little kitchen table. We had some girl talk which amounted to me talking and her shaking or nodding her head. I was getting ready to ask where Sarah was when she looked behind me and got a look of absolute terror on her face. I managed to duck, whirled around, grabbed a wooden spoon, and backed up when Mandy started screaming. The walker came at me because I was closer.

I yelled, "You have got to be kidding me," as I fended off its arms, then backed up to the table, threw the spoon, and grabbed a chair. Mandy continued to scream. "Keep screaming, Mandy girl," and pulled back when it grabbed my shirt. "What's with you guys? Ain't there little animals around you can terrorize?." I ducked again. "You're really pissing me off," then it pulled the chair from my grasp.

"Where the HELL is everyone?" I yelled, grabbed Mandy, and sidestepped behind the table as it reached for me. "When I say so, Mandy, run like hell." I didn't see if she heard me or not. I kept dodging the zombie until it decided to climb onto the table. I grabbed a skillet off the counter and

BONG! Right upside of the head. It had been soaking evidently because wet stuff went everywhere. Then I hit it again and yelled, "Run, Mandy," and she took off. The walker made like it was going to follow her until I bonged it upside the head again, then it came around the table at me.

I kept backing around the table until it was against the wall and then pushed the table as hard as I could. "Now, I got ya, shit head," and kept pushing the table. . Where was everyone? "How's it feel, puss face?" I was almost vibrating. I was so wound up. "I've had it with you all," pushing the table harder until suddenly it slipped, and the walker fell face first on the table. The table had cut it in half, and the top half crawled across the table after me. Its broken nails were gouging into the tabletop. whu=ile it tried to pull itself towards me. Yikes! Yuck, gross. I backed up slowly and looked for something to kill it with when its head blew up. I was deaf! A gun had gone off near my head, and I was deaf. I turned to run and ran into Mason.

He grabbed me as I yelled, "What took you so long?" My legs went out from under me. So much for adrenaline.

Mason pulled me up and then supported me into the great room, where he sat me gently on the couch. That's when the shaking started. He pulled me up against him and held me until I settled down, gently stroking my back. I let him as I nuzzled his neck. He smelled like fresh air, pine needles, and Mason's distinctive smell. The noises coming from the kitchen were the removal of the walker pieces. Ok, don't think about that...Then I heard a small voice crying, "Mama, mama, mama." Mandy? Mason helped me to Duke's room, and we saw Sarah cradling Mandy on her bed as she cried. "Mama, mama." Sarah smiled at me through the tears as she rocked Mandy. "Shhh, baby, mama's here," she whispered. "Mamas here." I started crying then, so Mason led me back to my couch. "Where was everyone?" I asked. "What took you so long?"

"It was only a couple of minutes, JD. We came running at the first scream." He gently caressed my back as he rocked me. "It just seemed longer when you're scared. We're trying to figure out where it came from. We cleared the whole building yesterday, but it must be hiding somewhere. We'll figure it out, ok? Just relax for now."

"I'll try. What is weighing on my mind is we slept here last night, and that thing was here. No problem, I can't do much more than breath right now anyway. If Mandy hadn't warned me, I'd be dead. I'm gonna stay right here till this whole place has been secured again. I can't handle another dance with the devil, so go, conquer... I'm done." With that, I put my feet on the table, leaned back, and left them to it. Mason stood and looked down at me, then turned and walked that fine ass out of the room. Sigh.

CHAPTER 9

Lacy came in and sat on the couch with me. "How ya doing?"
"Oh, just fine, and you?"
She smiled. "Great. The kitchen, however, is a mess. Lucky for me, Randy and Howard are cleaning up most of the gunk. I'll go in and finish up when they're done. Anything I can get ya?"
"Nope, can't think of a thing. Thanks so much for asking."
"Oh, think nothing of it." Lacy plays along just fine. "Mason has cleared this floor and is busy on the second floor. We think, however, it came from the little closet near the back door."
Puzzled, I turned toward her, "What little closet at the back door? I don't remember any little closet."
"That's what everyone is saying. Somehow, we missed it during the first sweep. It has brooms, mops and buckets, and such in it. Just enough room for a walker. It stinks in there too, and that's what makes us think it was in there." She slapped my knee, stood up, and hitched her shorts. "Well,

they're probably ready for me to mop the floor so Sarah can go back in there. I'll catch ya later."

I waved at her and settled back against the couch, listening to it creaking. Little closet hiding a walker that damned near killed me. Yeah, I can see that happening.

I thought of Mason, and there he was in my head. I thought, H*ow's it going, oh, mighty zombie hunter?* He laughed out loud, then thought back at me, *Making the world a safer place. Are these pink panties yours?*

I turned around on the couch and yelled, "Get your ass out of there."

Sarah came out and looked at me. "Out of where?" I heard Mason laugh again, and then a door slammed. "Mandy's sleeping, and Duke is staying with her while he works on his 'geek gear.' if she needs him. Did ya hear her, she said mama? She said you were brave and sorry she couldn't help."

"Dammit, Sarah, that little girl saved my bacon in there. She has nothing to be sorry for. Say, we got eggs now. How about we make a cake and celebrate her talking?"

"Sounds like a plan to me. I saw some tubs of frosting in there too. We could make it a chocolate cake with icing". She grabbed my arm, helped me stand, and walked us towards the kitchen. My legs were still a bit shaky, so we sat at the table while we waited for Lacy to finish, and then the three of us messed the kitchen up again.

Once Mandy started talking, not even the cake could stop her. No one bothered to tell her not to speak with her mouth full; we liked to hear her voice. We ate cake for the first time in over a year.

After that day, things calmed down and returned to almost normal. Duke got his cameras up and running and the wind generator going, so we had electricity but sparingly. Plans were made for a trip into town. We knew what we wanted but had trouble deciding who to send. We needed vital people to go but also stay and protect the lodge. The debate was a long, painful process, but by the end of the day, Mason, Randy, and Howard would go to town, leaving me, Duke, and Lacy to protect the lodge. Sarah was responsible for Mandy and Bubba.

The next day, after waving the crew away, I was pouting because I had wanted to go, boo hoo. The guys had done the sensible thing. And one part of me knew that but still. I was pouting. Walking the decks around the lodge, I scanned the horizon. I knew that Duke was doing the same thing with his cameras, but I needed to feel like I was productive. Poor me!

Sarah and Mandy had just gathered some eggs. The marked eggs had been put in a nest, and a hen was sitting on them. I knew Sarah would whip up something special tonight.

Something moved in my peripheral vision, and I turned. It was a dust cloud on the road leading here. As I watched it, it died down just about when Mandy came running around the corner. "Daddy says to hurry." I hurried.

"We've got company," he said, staring at the screen. I looked at the monitor and saw a very new, fancy, large truck. The truck was one of those four doors, king cab, dual tires, silver tool chest he-man types. He walked to the gate, squatted down, and looked intently at something. "What the hell is he doing?"

"Looking at tracks. I think he knows someone came in or went out."

We watched as he took out a handgun, checked the clip, then stuck it into the waistband of his jeans near the middle of his back, pulled his shirt out, and covered it all. He should've checked for the camera, too, damned fool.

"That ain't good." Duke whispered, "Sarah take Mandy and go to the RV, lock the door and hide in the bathroom." I thought she might argue, but she finally turned and left with Mandy, who looked back at us with the saddest eyes. "Now what?" I asked, picking up a rifle and ammo clip. "Play it by ear, but I know what I'll have to do to defend this place." He looked at me as the truck came around the bend and slowed as it approached the parking area.

"Let's go meet our guest."

We waited on the porch for the truck to come to a stop. The man inside just sat there for a moment, then put a smile on his face and opened the door. Duke held the rifle loosely and pointed at the ground, but I knew he was tightly wound. I stood with my rifle pointed at the guy. He has nothing on me.

He got out and stood with his hands raised. "Well, I didn't expect this. Do you mind?" he said, waving his hands.

"We mind. Keep 'em up". Duke said, raising the barrel of the rifle. He wasn't pointing at the guy, but it was close.

I just stood back and watched. I know this guy was having a problem with a little person holding a gun on him, and he looked at me and raised his eyebrows.

"Like he said," I replied.

"OK," he said, lowering his hands a bit. CLICK! And my gun was pointed and cocked.

"Now wait a minute, here. I come in peace," he yelled, raising his hands as high as they could. A sheen of sweat had appeared on his forehead. I don't think he's been in this position before.

"What do you want?" I asked

"Sanctuary?" He asked, looking from one of us to the other.

"No." Duke said, "Leave. Now." Motioning with his gun.

"Can't we talk about this first?

"No."

He looked at each of us again, turned to open the truck door, and swiftly grabbed the gun in his waistband. Two gunshots rang out, and Duke had hit him in the shoulder, and I blew his brains all over his fancy truck.

"Teach him to underestimate the power of a little person and a woman," I said and sighed. "Lacy, would you get the wheelbarrow for me, please?" I said to the air because I knew she was standing behind the window."

"I'll check his body, see who he is. Duke, I need you to monitor the cameras just in case he has friends." Duke nodded. Lacy and I were able to load his body into the wheelbarrow with a lot of wheezing. This guy was huge. Then we just stood there and looked at each other.

"I have no idea," I said in answer to her raised brows. "Damn, go to the RV and tell Sarah to come out. She's hiding there with Mandy." Lacy took off at a run while I stood next to the dead man and wondered when it had gotten to this point. He was part of the living. You don't kill the living unless they present a danger. We decided he was a danger while watching him at the gate. He never got the chance to create problems.

Lacy returned, and we stared at the man. "We need to get rid of this guy like he was never here. Help me load him in the truck."

After a considerable amount of swearing and dropping him twice, Sarah appeared, and we finally got him in his truck. "Why do they have to have those big ass tires? Crap, it must be four feet up." She sputtered, breathing heavily along with Lacy and me.

Once I recovered enough to speak, I asked Lacy if she could drive the four-wheeler. "Sure, JD, I'll go get it."

"What ya got in mind?" Sarah asked.

I pointed to the top of the nearest mountain; it sported several cell phone towers and satellite dishes. "There's a nice drop-off on the other side and a halfway decent road to the top. I'll drive the body off the cliff, no more problem. Lacy can drive me back."

"Why don't we just haul him up and throw him off the cliff? Why ruin this nice truck?"

"If he has friends, and I kinda doubt it, but just in case, I don't want them to show up and recognize his truck and not find him. This way, if they find him crashed at the bottom of the cliff, they'll think he got drunk and drove off the cliff in the dark or something." She nodded and then headed back inside. I checked with Duke, and he said it was clear, so I drove to the top of the mountain with Lacy close behind. Then we wrangled him around until he was in the driver's seat, put the transmission in neutral, and pushed him over the side between us. The noise was horrible, and dust flew everywhere. We drove back to the gate, gave the thumbs up to the camera, and went home.

It wasn't till the next day, around noon, that I got a thought from Mason. *We're about to approach the gate,* and after a few seconds, we could hear Mandy yelling, "They're back," repeatedly. We joined her on the front porch, where she jumped around and squealed. I wanted to, but badass zombie killers don't do that. So we waited as three semis and a truck rounded the bend. What? *We have a new member, so be nice,* Mason thought at me.

"What the hell," Duke said, proving he could count.

"This better be good," I said.

They stopped in the lane, single file. Men started to pile out of the trucks. Lacy ran at Randy and nearly threw them both to the ground in her excitement. Mason, Howard, and a stranger proceeded to the front porch.

He was tall, over 6 feet, and built like a football player. He was also bald with brown eyes, a square chin, and a full mouth. His lips smiled at me, and I realized I was staring. Clearing my throat, I looked at Mason.

"We were having a bit of a problem but not with walkers. There is a militia group protecting the town and wasn't happy we got a semi full of wind turbines. Took exception to us actually, and Flynn helped us out."

"What were you doing there, Mr. Flynn? Were you part of the militia? If you were, you have a long walk back to town."

"That's what Mason said, too, but sending me back after I know where you live is a bad idea." Duke straightened the rifle a bit more.

"No need for that. I was there before they came. They showed up one day and decided they wanted to run things. Poorer bunch of commandos I've ever seen. They lose a member every day because they don't know what they're doing. I broke off from them two months ago just to survive. I'm doing better on my own. However, they will consider me a deserter if they catch me."

"So why are you here?" I asked

"Your people are the best equipped, best organized I've been around. You know what you want, plan how to get it, and then get in and out. I think you have the best chance of surviving this crap than anyone, and there is safety in numbers."

I looked at Mason. *Do you trust him?* I thought. He nodded.

Looking at Flynn, I said, "You know someone driving a large, silver Ram, tall, and carries a

pistol in the jeans waistband?"
"Yeah, that's Jerry. He's mean as hell, shoots first, and asks questions later. He went out yesterday to check out the neighborhood. Why?"
"He showed up here, drew on us, and we took care of him. You have a problem with that?"
Flynn looked at Mason, who just stared at me. His mind was blank, but I knew that wouldn't last long.
"If he's dead, then you just did the world a favor. He's been asking for it a long time. How did you get the jump on him?"
I smiled, "We didn't, Flynn. We just killed him cause we didn't like the way he looked. Come in and tell us what you brought us."
The smile died from Flynn's face as he followed us into the dining room. He got a good look at the lights on in the dining room and turned to Mason. "You have electricity?" Mason pointed out the window to the wind turbine. "Yep, but we needed more, so that's why we brought back FOUR more." He said pointedly to Duke, whose face lit up.
"Damn, Mason, you the man."
"Remember that old man when it comes time to set them up."

"Old man, is it? I won't forget that. I'm back at the cameras. Come on, Mandy girl, dad needs a hand."

Flynn watched the duo walk out. Then noticed Sarah coming from the kitchen with a platter of cold fried chicken in one hand and a bowl of fresh tomatoes in the other. Then he saw the chocolate cake on the buffet. "Something on your mind, Flynn?" I asked, grinning at Mason.

"More like it's on my stomach."

"Let's eat then, and you can tell us what we needed three semi's for."

Later that day, Sarah had a fancy new fridge, one pallet of flour, sugar (brown and white), rice, and pasta. There was wrapping paper for meat and zip lock baggies. There was ammo of every kind, a couple of cases of bazookas, and several machine guns. When I looked at Mason, he just shrugged. OK, well, we're armed now.

Just about dusk, Mandy came in on tiptoes and held a finger to her mouth. "Look out the window," she whispered. We did and then ran in every direction. A whole herd of deer was milling around in the yard. I got the bow, cocked it, and after shaking my head at Flynn, I snuck out to the deck. Picking out the biggest buck, which looked like a 5x5, I killed him, which made Mandy very unhappy.

I let the men take care of the deer while I tried to console Mandy. That didn't go over very well, so I let Sarah handle it. Lacy had disappeared with Randy, so I hoped they brought back a pallet of condoms. Grabbing a chicken leg, I sat at the table. I nursed a bottle of raspberry tea until the men started to filter in, putting the front and back quarters and tenderloin on the counter. Bubba was standing at one end of the counter, on his hind legs begging. Howard scooped him up and wandered into the other room, saying something about dog farts and deer meat.

Sarah came in and began to clean the meat. I joined her, and we cut and wrapped the deer, putting most of it in the new freezer of the fridge and some we planned to have the next day for dinner.

Mason left with Flynn and showed Flynn around. He chose a bedroom in the basement because he planned to take the night guard duty, and sleeping in the dark basement would be better and quieter. I agreed.

Tomorrow the trailers would be emptied except for one, and the others would be lined up to start our fence. The south of the lodge had the cliff wall, which ran southwest and ended at a ravine on the property's western edge. So those sections were OK. We started the fence at the end of the ravine nearest the road. Then we planned the wall to run along the road to the gate and put a solar-powered remote-controlled gate. One hundred six feet (or two 53-foot trailers) of the fence began at the ravine's edge. We would need many more trailers, but the cameras would do the job now. Howard was busy getting the snowmobiles ready for the winter. There were four of them, and they had their garage. There was a ranch house at the intersection where the paved road ended, and the gravel road to our place started. Howard proposed to take a truck with a snow plow there and two snowmobiles so we could get in and out during the winter.

Mason, Flynn, and Duke started work on the wind generators while we made plans for the winter. I wanted the windows covered with plastic, so we needed a trailer full of plastic and tape. Another list was created.

We set up one of the rooms near the kitchen as a clinic. I was satisfied with the results. Flynn seemed to be a hard worker and had some noteworthy ideas. He explained that he was a demolition expert and an Iraq war veteran, and that was it. Flynn handled the cameras at night and didn't complain. We didn't see him during the day while he slept, so there wasn't a lot of interaction with him. When he did stay up to help, he was friendly enough. He and Mason became fast friends, so life settled a bit, and we let it.

CHAPTER 10

The sun woke me around 10 a.m. Mason, Flynn, and Howard had gone to town. We had chosen a different city this time, hoping they wouldn't run into trouble. I expected them back sometime today, hopefully with at least three trailers. They each drove a semi out, so all they had to do was fill the trailers, hook up and go. We've had a wonderful week since they got back with Flynn. That was fine with me. I could almost breathe easily and was starting to relax.

That is, until one morning, when I opened the bathroom door, a very naked Randy was getting out of our shower. Crap! I squeezed my eyes shut, turned, closed my door, went to the window seat, and sat down. Crap!

Ok, so now what do I do? I put on my new satin robe, walked out into the hall, and when I started to knock on Lacy's door, it flew open, and we nearly collided. I grabbed her hand, pulled her back to my room, and shut the door. She went to the window seat, sat, and opened her mouth.

"Before you say anything, are you using condoms? Cause if you aren't, I'll kick your ass."

Blushing, she started to say something, and I cut her short again. "The next thing is I can't deal with a naked Randy under any circumstances, so you both are moving to the south suite...it has a sitting room and private bath. Today, you're doing this cause I can't deal with a naked Randy. I just can't. I won't either. I don't have to, and it ain't happening again".

I was repeatedly pacing from the door to her and then back to the door. When I returned to her, she grabbed my hands and stopped me.

"We are using condoms, JD, we aren't children, and we don't want any for a while. Relax, I was going to ask about the honeymoon suite, but I was putting it off. I didn't know how you'd react. Now that's settled, I want to talk about you".

"Me? What's wrong with me? Nothing, that's what. I'm fine now that we have a home, and I don't have to worry about turning a corner and running into a walker every time I leave the house. So you don't have anything to talk to me about, that's what."

"Wow. Well." She started to stand up. "Ok, well, now may not be the time."

"Time? for what? Just sit your little ass back down and tell me what you're talking about".

"Well, we, Randy and me, noticed that you and Mason are, well, are...friendly."

"And just what is wrong with us being friendly?"

"Nothing, but well, Flynn has been showing an interest when you're around, and Mason has noticed, and we, Randy and me, thought maybe you might be interested in Flynn too, so well, you have to decide."

"Decide? Decide what?" I was not tracking well at all.

"Well, which one do you want."

"Want? What? What the hell are you talking about?"

She looked at me like I had grown two heads. Mason and Flynn? They aren't interested in me, are they? I mean, Mason kissed me a couple of times, and I've admired his ass whenever I had the chance, and Flynn's ass was fine too but, oh crap! I'm screwed.

I sat down on the window seat with Lacy. Moaning, I put my face in my hands and rocked back and forth. She put her arm around me, and I thought I heard a giggle come from her. I looked up quickly, but that's when she got up and walked to the door. "We'll start moving our stuff to the other room. Seeing his butt is not something I want you to do either. Although, it is a fine one. Relax, I think you have a bit longer before they start dueling over you".

I stared at the door long after she left. Then shaking myself like a dog, I took my stuff, went to Mason's room, and showered. Drying my hair as I stumbled back to my room, I thought about Mason and Flynn. When did Flynn become an issue? He's nice enough. He even pulled out my chair for me once, and he will hold the door for me every once in a while, but he's just being nice. Right? Crap! Tying my shoes, I decided not to think about it again. I wanted to take the four-wheeler out and check the grounds. The cliff wall behind the lodge tapered down to a ravine, and I wanted to check behind it.

I drank my coffee and stared out the window contemplating Mason and Flynn. The noises told me Lacy and Randy were moving into the honeymoon suite, and from the laughing and giggling, it was going fine. I smiled at the thought of having my bathroom again. A flash from the north caught my attention, but when I stared long and hard at it, I didn't see anything else.

I took my coffee into Duke's Den, as we were calling it. Sarah started it, and it had stuck. He glanced up when I walked in, then hooked the small stool next to him with his foot and pulled it out for me to sit. He smiled when I put the mug full of coffee in front of him.

"What's up?" he said, playing with the gate camera.

"Not much. I thought I saw a reflection north of the lodge and wondered if you caught it too."

"Yep, it was just that once. I don't know what it was. You going to check it out?"

"Might as well. I was gonna check behind the cliff wall and see what's there. There's a road that runs around there so someone was using it for some reason."

"Take someone with you when you do, Randy maybe."

"No, no, that's alright. I'll take Lacy; she can handle herself."

Duke snuck a look at me and raised one eyebrow. (How do you raise one eyebrow? I've tried it, and it's like they're both connected). "Ok, you should be ok. I might use Randy in my helicopter experiment."

"Oh, are you that close?"

"If it works, I'll give you a special viewing when you get back."

"Sounds good," Mussing his hair and him hollering "Hey" behind me, I walked back to the kitchen to await Lacy. Mandy was at the table, so I quickly sat beside her with my back to the wall. I learned from the last time.

Bumping shoulders with her, she smiled and offered me part of her pop tart. She had declined to eat the deer, and I hoped she would eventually, but she was holding out so far.

Sarah was busy putting together a stew in the crock pot. I wasn't about to mention the deer meat in front of Mandy, but it would cook all day, and the guys would have a good meal when they returned. She had already started the fresh bread, and the smells in the kitchen brought back good memories of my childhood.

"Lacy and I are going to the ravine and checking things out as soon as she and Randy move into the honeymoon suite. I found him all-natural in my shower this morning, so I strongly suggested they move today."

"What's 'all natural' mean?" Mandy asked around her pastry. She asked many questions, and it seemed like nothing got past her.

"Ask your dad," Sarah said as she stirred the stew. Mandy jumped down and ran to the front room, followed closely by Bubba. Sarah covered the casserole and then sat at the table.

"Now that you have Lacy in a safe place, what about you? You deserve to be happy too, ya know? Mason and Flynn are both great guys, although we don't know much about Flynn yet."

"You too? Geez, just this morning, Lacy nailed me with this crap." I got up and started for the door. "You have to choose, or they're gonna get in a fight," she said softly.

"I haven't thought about it, but I will now since that's all anyone can talk about."

"Do it soon. It isn't fair to them."

"Oh, for heaven's sake," then stomped to the barn. I don't give a damn if it's fair to them or not. Let them beat each other up over the honor of holding the door for me—what a crock. I started up the four-wheeler and tooted the horn for Lacy. While I waited, I cocked my bow and set it aside. Soon Lacy came bouncing out, and after locking her rifle into its slot in front of her, we took off.

She talked a mile a minute. Randy this and Randy that. I headed to the spot where I thought I had seen the reflection that morning and tried to tune her out. The terrain was bumpy, and the going was slow, but we finally stopped at the ravine and

got out. Looking down into the ravine, I was surprised at what I saw. Several walkers were milling around in the creek at the bottom.
They saw us and attempted to climb the ravine to get to us. Lacy started for her gun, but I stopped her and reached for the bow. I killed six before I ran out of arrows. I told Duke that he would hear a gunshot and that Lacy would kill the last one. I was glad the spring ran downhill away from us but it bothered me that they were contaminating the water.
"Well, crap," I said, got the rope out from behind the seat, and tied it to yellow pine growing near the ravine's edge.
"You're kidding. You can't go down there."
"They have to be moved away from the creek, Lacy. They're contaminating the water."
"So, the water runs the other way. What do we care?"
"Lacy, what if a family lives somewhere down the creek, just trying to survive like us? Do you want them to drink that water? Keep a look out for me, and if you see a walker, shoot em in the head like I taught you".
I started down the rope, and since it had been a while since I had repelled down a cliff, I more or

less slid to the bottom. When I got to the bottom, I took a minute to look around, rubbing my hands together from the rope burn I got. Then I started to haul bodies as far from the creek as possible. By the time I was done, I was sweaty and tired.

"Oh shit, JD, get up here right now. Now. Hurry. Dammit, move your ass!!"

I ran, grabbed the rope, and banged into the bank while trying to get a foothold in the loose rock. "Shoot" I yelled.

"I can't. You're in the way". Crap, I thought as I tried to climb up the cliff, but my feet kept slipping. Suddenly a hand clamped around my ankle and started to pull, and I felt the rope slide from my sweaty hands. I swayed and kicked with my other foot while trying to hang on. Then a loud shot rang out, and the pressure on my foot disappeared. I just hung there for a minute and then worked my way back up to the top.

Lacy helped me climb the last foot, and we sat on the ground.

"And I thought it was getting boring around here," I said between pants. "If that dead bastard is in the creek, I'll send a letter of apology to the folks downstream." Then we started laughing as we shakily climbed into the mule.

CHAPTER 11

I've been secretly compiling a list. Not just any old list. No, sir, not me. A Christmas list. I'm going on our next trip to town, although no one knew that yet. It couldn't be helped, I needed some personal things anyway, and I'm going. The guys have been putting me off whenever they go into town for some reason or another. I can drive a semi, so...No more. I am going and of story.

I wish Duke could go, but he can't drive a semi and wouldn't be much help picking and choosing items. Sarah and Lacy seemed content to sit here, and I'm just afraid after a very long winter. they will be nuts or drive the rest of us crazy. I think she needs to get out of the lodge, but I can't for the life of me figure out a way.

Winter was fast approaching, and we needed at least one more run. The fence was nearly done, and a wooden corral was built for Casey, the cow

(Mandy named her). Hay was restacked in the area north of the corral for a wind break, and the wood was restacked all over the wraparound porch. Wood was up to the bottom of the windows and up each side about 6 feet. We still had enough to stack on the decks between the rails.

We had five wind turbines running with extra batteries and parts and a trailer full of more parts. Duke believes in being prepared. There were water pump parts, two additional water heaters, several electric heaters for individual uses, and electric stock water heaters for the cow, hogs, and chickens.

The clinic had been moved to Howard's room. Since it had an attached library and bath, he graciously gave it up to move into Randy's old room. The clinic held an exam table, heart monitors, iv drips, cabinets of antibiotics, pain meds. You name it, we had it and were learning how to operate it. We learned to take blood pressures and temperatures, give injections, and stitch cuts. Our medical library was pretty good with diagnostic dictionaries so that we could look up the big words. I sincerely hoped we never had to use it. We even had a small area for animals like Bubba.

The freezer was stocked with venison, chicken, and pork. Flynn and Mason ran into a small herd of wild hogs, and we spent several long days processing meat. The survival books gave ideas on how to render fat, Yuk. We had three live hogs in a small wooden corral we planned to fatten them up. I gave the livestock over to Randy's gentle touch, and he seemed to flourish.

The trailer wall was finished with a steel reinforced, solar-powered, electrified, remote-controlled gate. If anyone tried to climb over or move it, they would be fried. Another one of Duke's inventions. He installed so many cameras that the monitors had to be numbered to keep up with them. He knew what was where and you knew better than to touch anything. He was the one who found some deer on the other side of the mountain with his helicopter. I took some nice pictures with it too, which we haven't heard the end of yet.

I took everyone aside individually and asked if they wanted to pick up something for someone for Christmas and to make a list. So far, I had a list from everyone but Mason, and even Mandy got in on the act. She was asking for a pretty sweater for mama and a ball cap made with Hawaiian material for daddy.

I'd checked in the attic and found tons of Christmas decorations and wrapping paper. So all I had to pick up was tape. We used a lot of tape, and lacy and I had already picked out the tree, so all I needed to do was go shopping.

We had a snowstorm roar for two days, and I thought I was too late, but the sun came out and melted everything and warmed up nicely. The guys got together and started planning a trip for the next day. I pulled up a chair, sat, and smiled at them. A collective sigh arose, and I steeled myself for the fight ahead.

Before anyone had a chance to say anything, I blurted out, "I'm going if I have to take the RV" It was mine, so I knew they couldn't stop me. They knew it too.

"Ok," Mason said, throwing up his hands. The others just smiled, and I knew they had planned to let me go before I had opened my mouth. Smartasses!! I'll show them.

I was waiting on the porch in the rocking chair early the following day. Sipping coffee from a travel mug, I admired the view, slowly rocking, waiting for someone to come out. I was too

excited to eat anything, but I knew the others would, if for no other reason than to piss me off. Wrong! Nothing was going to upset me today. Flynn came out first with his travel mug and leaned against the railing, looking at the sunrise.
"Sure is pretty here." He said.
"Yep"
"The prettiest place I've ever been"
"Uh, huh."
"Hate to leave, it's so pretty."
"We leaving, or are ya gonna talk all day?" asked Mason as he barreled out the door in front of Howard. Randy was watching the lodge with Duke and Lacy. We planned to return tonight, so I had on my racing shoes. We piled into the semis, me in the truck with Howard. Mason and Flynn hesitated like they wanted to say something, then got in their rigs. Howard seemed surprised at first, then just grinned as we waited for the air in the tanks to build up.
Duke signaled that all the explosive devices were disabled and the gate was opening, so we pulled out. I was so excited that I started taking pictures of everything. When we hit the interstate, I was surprised to see most of the traffic roadblocks were cleared, and we had a straight shot to town.

Although, to be fair, it was a city. Malls and warehouses were along the interstate. I indicated the local Wal-Mart store, and we pulled into the lot and around to the docks. Trailers were parked at both docks, so Howard backed up to one while Flynn the other. Mason hurriedly hooked up both. The weapons in hand, we opened the door and went inside. Mason locked the door and, at my look, said, "We've already cleared the building, and this way, it stays clear. Go shopping but take someone with you."

Flynn grabbed a pallet truck and a pallet, loaded an empty box five feet square onto the pallet, and motioned me to follow him. Ok, it beats the cart all to hell.

We entered the store near the frozen food section, which was disappointing and smelly. We located the shoe section, and the shopping was on. I picked out winter boots, coats, and all the other winter accruements.

By the time I had made the rounds, I had filled four pallets with stuff, and my butt was dragging. I spent some time at the jewelry department for Lacy's engagement rings, but I couldn't decide which ones to get, so I got them all. I mean, really, why not? Flynn was taking his time returning, so I got watches too and was headed to the feminine hygiene aisle, and yep, you got it, ran into a walker, well, almost. It was lying on the floor, dragging what was left of his legs and leaving a slime trail behind him like a slug, only a different color.

I'm backing up slowly when I back into a solid wall of muscle. I thought Mason until I caught his scent and knew I was in trouble.

"Well, what have we got here, Dell? It looks like a little pussy has slipped in for personal shopping. Isn't that right, sweetheart, doing some shopping?" No, I was standing on my head whistling Dixie. Fool!

His arms were like steel as he squeezed me to him and his breath told me he had spent some time in the alcohol aisle. Maybe too much time, although I could see where it would take some effort to find soap and deodorant.

"Dell" walked up behind the walker and cleaved his head in two with a machete putting the thing out of its misery. I briefly thought, *I wonder if they have feelings.*

Dell was about my height but a good 350 pounds. He must have forgotten to use his deodorant that morning cause he smelled almost worse than the walker. Stepping over the thing on the floor, he wiped the blood from the machete on his pants. Yuck! and shuffled over to us.

"I ain't had me no strange pussy in months," he said, and his breath made me turn my head away. I wondered again if he'd had familiar pussy, ever. "No shit, dead meat, you probably couldn't run fast enough to catch any." He backhanded me hard enough to split my lip, then 'the vise' grabbed a hand full of hair and growled, "You better be nice, bitch, if you want us to keep you alive for a while."

All this time, I'm thinking to Mason, *Get your ass in here now, and shoot these assholes. aisle 7, feminine hygiene. Where the hell are you?*

I'm coming around the isle now. When I tell you to, drop.

I said to 'the vise,' "Let me go now, and I promise to kill you quickly." He laughed like I knew he would. *"DROP,"* I heard, and I did. I went limp, and I don't think 'the vise' thought I'd do that. A surprised look came over "Dell," and he crumpled to the floor on top of the walker with a large knife sticking out of his back. 'The vise' followed soon after.

"Dammit, why do I always end up on the floor

and bleeding?" I mumbled, grabbed some sanitary wipes from the shelf beside me, and tore open the package. Mason helped me, and Flynn walked up and kicked 'the vise' in the head. "Assholes." Then he shot each of them in the head with my bow before handing it to me as he walked by. Shaking his head at me, he winked. Then he took a wipe and cleaned a spot on my cheek.

"You missed a spot, Brat." Then he gently rubbed his knuckles over my cheek.

"Almost done here?" asked Mason, sounding a bit put out. I jumped because I was a little distracted by Flynn. "A... yeah, I mean, sure, almost, this section, few minutes." I shook myself and looked at the 'vise' as I held the wipes to my lips. Then I looked at him and was violently pissed. I started kicking him as hard as I could and, with every kick, yelled, "Stupid! Asshole! Idiotic! Dumbass! Shithead!" Mason pulled me back and then looked from him to me. When I saw the expression on his face, I yelled "MEN!!" at him, turned, and ran head first into Flynn. He threw his hands up in surrender and quickly stepped to one side as I stomped back to the rear of the store, snatching a ball cap with a Hawaiian motif off a shelf as I walked by.

Howard looked at me and started to say something but looked behind me and quickly shut his mouth. I climbed into the semi and pouted as I watched the men talk in whispers and nod, then headed to their semis. Howard got in, quickly glanced in my direction, then started the rig, and we pulled out. I sat there with a feminine pad against my mouth and was silent. It was quiet as we drove back home. My lip had quit bleeding but felt like it was as big as a grapefruit.

Before I knew it, I was crying, and I stared out the window and let the tears flow. Howard was very quiet as he handed me a handkerchief, and I sniffled all the way home. My trailer was unhooked next to the school bus and left locked. The other trailers were backed up to the side of the lodge to be unloaded in the next few days.

I went inside and straight to my room, ignoring the questions and strange looks. I'd let the boys answer the questions; I needed time alone.

The "vise" was Dean Connelly, who had worked at the lodge one summer when I was visiting. We quickly became an item, and I fell in love. He didn't, but he kept at me till he got in my pants, then dropped me. I heard later he was keeping a tally on how many girls he could screw during the summer. He had some bet with his best friend, and from what I heard, he won by one point. No one knew about it, and it wasn't something I was particularly proud of either. Being made a fool isn't easy to accept, and I guess I still hadn't accepted it yet, but now Dean was dead, and I was glad. He would have known that I was living at the lodge now.

  When we met, I was living in NW Montana. He would have found us, and I couldn't have handled the fact that it would have been my fault. He was dead; it was time for me to move on. But not till I was over being mad. It was right; I was enjoying it, and by God, I was going to do it till I quit. So there.

Hunger, more than anything else, got me out of my room that night. I was in the kitchen digging through the fridge when Lacy came in. I straightened up as she hugged me.

"You ok?" she asked

"Yeah, or will be. Seem to say that a lot anymore."

She turned me toward her and winced when she saw my face.

"Looks that bad, huh? Fat bastard could backhand. But no more" I threw my hands up, waving a chicken leg. "Cause that fat bastard is a greasy old lard spot right in front of the vaginal cream."

"I was just wondering...what?" Lacy gaped at me. I reached out and slowly raised her chin until her mouth closed, then patted her cheek. I grabbed the chicken and a soda and went to the kitchen table where I sat, with my back to the wall. Yep, not over that one yet.

She finally turned around and looked at me, then shook her head and got herself a pop.

"So, you going to tell me who the dead guy on the floor is? Or how you mouthed off to the fat bastard causing him to backhand you? Or better yet, how you kicked the shit out of the dead guy on the floor after he was dead and couldn't appreciate it?"

"Listen, sweetie, you'll have to settle on one question and stay there cause I don't want to talk about it. However, I've decided to answer one question because you're my favorite sister. So which is it?" Damn, that chicken was good. Wonder what kind of spice that is.

"I'm your only sister. The dead guy on the floor".

"Shit, I was hoping it was the fat guy who backhanded me."

"Concentrate here, JD, who was the dead guy on

the floor? Mason said you kicked him and called him names. Who was he?"

I sighed and put my chicken down. Then I washed it down with the pop and told her the story of Dean. I didn't hold anything back and was pissed off all over again when I was done. I grabbed a thigh and ripped a hunk off, and while I chewed and looked at her.

I smacked her fingers when she reached over to get a wing. "You had yours."

"So that's it? You kicked the shit out of him, oh dear, that brings up an awful image, anyway, not because he was going to rape you but because he screwed you over four years ago?" I raised my eyebrows at her and saw the light bulb over her head.

"That rat bastard! He thought he was gonna get to screw you over twice? Dickless, spineless, motherless, sumbitch!" Yep, my Lacy could cuss, and it made me proud. She started pacing back and forth until Randy came in the room, winced when he saw my face, then frowned when he saw Lacy pacing. She noticed and growled at him while I sat silently chewing my chicken like it was the most natural thing in the world. He slowly backed out of the room. Well, maybe he's ok after all. It takes a wise man to know when to retreat. She sat next to me and put her arm around me, patting me gently on the knee. "It's all right, sis. You rant all you want, deserve it, and I might help. No wonder you were so mad when you got home. I would be too." I chewed the last meat off the bone and put my head on her shoulder.

"I'll be ok; I just had a lot of adrenaline that had no place to go. But the thought of him lying there, dead, his head all kicked in and pissed pants right in front of the condoms is much better than the picture I had of him before."

"Now tell me what the guys said about these two morons and if they had any friends there." I got up and put my things away, and washed my hands. Mason was taking so long to help me because he was fighting his battle with two other morons outside. After he finished them, he came running to help me. Howard had to deal with one guy he said was an Elvis wants to be, but that the guy was probably talking to Elvis now. There were five of them, but they weren't sure if there were any more. We left too quick to find out.

It seemed like all the guns going off were attracting a lot of walkers, which the guys could see in the rearview mirrors. I shrugged as if I

could care less, hugged her, and said how tired I was. I went to bed. I took an aspirin because my face hurt, and my lip started bleeding while eating, but I didn't care. I crawled into bed, curled around my body pillow, and dreamed about giant roaches chasing me with a bikini top locked in their pinchers.
Don't ask.

CHAPTER 12

Several weeks after the last trip, we woke up to snow. Several inches were on the ground while a steady, slow, feathery snow was gently falling. The quiet enfolded me when I stepped out to get some wood, and I stood and listened. Everything else was doing the same thing, it seemed. Even the birds were quiet, and you could almost hear the snow fall. I could see my breath in the cold, so I hurried up and went back inside.

The furnace worked well, but we used the great room's fireplace anyway. Something about a fire on a snowy day just seemed to soothe the soul. You could almost believe it was several years ago when your biggest worry was rising gas prices and the next new electronic gadget. Sitting with your stocking feet propped on the coffee table, you could feel the warmth tickle your toes. The sounds of crackling wood and someone in the kitchen rattling pots and pans brought a smile to my face. Texas was a long time ago.

I padded into the dining room and grabbed a cup of coffee. Inhaling deeply, Then I wandered into the kitchen. Sarah was kneading dough while a sleepy-eyed Mandy sat swinging her feet and waiting for breakfast. She also sat with her back to the wall, but I don't think it was from any conscious thoughts of the walkers. She'd drawn a happy face in the dew on her glass of orange juice. I scooted onto the seat next to her and bumped her shoulder with mine. She giggled like she was supposed to. Before I could say anything, Mason slipped into my head.

Hey, smarty pants, why don't you come here and let me show you something special?

I choked.

Coffee spewed from my nose all over the table and my shirt. Tears ran down my face as little Mandy beat me on the back with both hands. Sarah brought me a paper towel and added her pounding to Mandy's. I could hear Mason chuckling in my mind.

Once I had learned to breathe again and assured Sarah that I was fine, I excused myself with a fresh cup of coffee to my room. Before I closed the door, I glanced across the great room area to Flynn's room as he walked by his doorway in his undershorts.

I almost choked again. My God, that man was okay. Broad shoulders tapered over six-pack abs to the smallest waist I've ever seen on a man. The muscles in his thighs rippled with each step. I just stood there staring, like a teeny bopper, probably drooling down my tee shirt if the truth is known. Mason's door opened, and he stepped out. Then he saw me and stopped, and I narrowed my eyes at him, stuck my nose in the air, and slammed my door. Smartass!

No sooner had I sat on the window seat to enjoy the view and my coffee when a knock sounded on my door, and I ignored it. It came again, then once more. "Come on, open the door, sweetie. I want to tell you something."

"Go away, sweetie," I shouted, "I'm busy."

"No, you aren't," he shouted back.

There went my solitude. Might as well let him come in now.

"'Come in then."

"I'm sorry about the choking. I didn't mean for that to happen. I have something outside my window I want to show you. Please?"

I looked at him a minute, and he did look sorry, so I thought it couldn't hurt.

He led me around the great room and into his room. Then we walked over to the window and looked out.

"What do you see?" he asked.

"I don't have the energy for this morning, Mason. Just tell me whatever it is you want me to know."

"Look over to the northeast corner, near the orange trailer."

So I looked. At first, I didn't see anything but snow, then something caught my eye, and I looked. I turned to say something to Mason, and he was there holding a pair of binoculars.

Smartass! I took a second look at the trailer and saw it. A walker stood in waist-deep snow, slowly rocking back and forth. He didn't look like he was going anywhere soon.

"How the hell did he get there? I thought we had the fence tight enough no one could get through." I said, squinting through the glasses.

"I know, right? But we must find the spots they can get through and fix them."

"Well, we have to take care of it. We can't have him wandering around the place even if he is stuck at the moment."

I'll get the snowmobile ready after I tell Flynn."

He turned to leave when I grabbed his arm.

"I'm going on this little trip. Flynn goes every time, and now it's my turn. You guys act as if you are hooked at the hip, for Pete's sake. Let me change into my snowmobile suit, and we'll take care of this thing."

I turned to go, and he grabbed my arm. When I turned back to see what he wanted, he kissed me again. One of those with the tongue, the toes curling, and the warm feeling down low. When he released me, I licked my lips and smiled. He turned me around and gently shoved me toward the door. I just stood there when I had closed my bedroom door. He'd done it to me again! What the hell was wrong with me? Okay, I knew my problem, but I wouldn't think about it today. Tomorrow was soon enough.

Finally remembering what I was doing, I changed into my purple suit and grabbed my purple striped gloves. I hadn't used them yet; they felt stiff and smelled new. My color-coordinated boots of light and dark purple waited by the back door. I guess Mason had explained to Sarah where we were going because she handed me my knit cap and smiled. I stuffed it into my pocket, grabbed my plum-colored helmet off the table by the door, and headed out to the sound of the snowmobile before anyone could say anything.

I saw Flynn watching through the dining room window as we drove around the back deck. He didn't look happy, and I smiled and waved at him as we roared away. I'd forgotten something important about snowmobiles; they vibrate under your butt. After a few minutes, I had to shift in my seat.

"What's wrong" Mason shouted over the engine.

"Nothing, just drive." I was glad he couldn't see my red face.

The walker began to strain toward us when we got close enough for him to see and hear us. Since we were on a big old noisy machine, I didn't see any sense in trying to be quiet, so I took out the shotgun, And blew his head off. Overkill big time.

"Were you planning on shooting big game with this thing? Crap, there's brains for miles." He said.

"There you go exaggerating again. Every time I turn around, you are defaming my character."

"What the hell are you talking about? I don't defame your character; for Pete's sake, you don't have any character.

"I didn't say I had a good character, but thanks for that assessment. That coffee thing was an accident, and you know it. I can't help it if you have a dirty mind."

"Dirty mind? You! You caveman, you have the dirty mind. 'Let me show you something special.' What the hell is that if not the product of a dirty mind?"

Lacy jumped into my mind with both feet. *Get back now, JD. Howard just got back from the roadhouse with an unconscious girl.*

"We gotta go," we both said at the same time. I guess he got that message too, and I'll think about that tomorrow also.

Our minds jumped and skitted back and forth, worse than the machine we were riding on, all the way back to the lodge. I didn't even notice the vibrations this time.

Skidding to a stop at the back door, I dismounted and ran up the steps tripping on the last one. No, I didn't fall. When I hit the kitchen floor, the snow on my boots acted like skis, and I slid across the floor. Didn't fall that time either. Go figure.

Lacy ran into me in the dining room with my slippers and made me peel myself out of the suit and boots and into the warm, dry slippers. I ran into the clinic in my sweat suit to find everyone there.

"Clear the room till we find out if she's infected.

Lacy, would you warm some chicken broth? Duke, would you ask Mandy to help Lacy? Let's get these clothes off, and I need something to tie her down for the time being—just hands and feet for now. Whew, we need to clean her up too. She smells to high heaven.

Sarah had a pair of shears and was busy cutting the clothes away. We were looking for bite marks but would have to remove all her clothes to find out.

"We'll need a heater in here since we are stripping her. Mason, would you get a basin of warm water and disinfectant soap from the bathroom? Flynn, I have some big wooly, warm socks in my dresser. Would you get them for me?

We spent the next hour stripping, cleaning, and getting her into something warm. We didn't find any bite marks anywhere. In the meantime, Howard told us how he had seen her huddled in the roadhouse where we kept the snow plow and snowmobile. We check it several times weekly to ensure nothing was tampered with.

He saw footprints leading to the back of the house and investigated, finding the girl in the bedroom, unconscious under a mountain of blankets. When he didn't find bite marks on her, he decided to bring her back.

At first, we were concerned that she might turn, but after a while, we took care of her as if she was one of us. I thought she was just exhausted, and after a good rest, she should be okay. She was really pretty, with stubble for hair. We figured she shaved it for sanitary reasons, and getting bugs out of long hair is hard. She was skinny, but that was expected, her fingernails were split and caked, and slight frostbite was evident on her fingers, toes, and tips of her ears and nose.

We took turns overnight sitting with her. She didn't move or make a noise. Bubba had taken to sleeping on top of the covers between her legs. Howard said he tried to make her well and would leave her alone when she got better. Flynn seemed taken with staying with her too. Not sure what was going on there, but I left him to it.

Just after noon the next day, she started to wake up. We warmed the broth up again and made her some hot tea. I was with her when she slowly opened her eyes.

"You're okay, with friends. You've been ill, and you'll be okay now. Just rest. When you're ready, we have tea and broth for you."

She looked at me, then around the room. 'Safe,'

she whispered and went back to sleep.
When she awoke an hour later, she said she was ready for the broth. It didn't stay down, but I expected that. We tried the tea, and she tackled some more broth again when it stayed down. Bubba lay down with her again, and they both slept the afternoon away. She ate some more broth and crackers, drank two cups of tea that night, and then slept through the night.
Two days later, she was walking with the help of Flynn, and he was at her side constantly, which was cause for a lot of speculation.
She was seated at the dining table when I came in, Flynn at her side.
"What's your name anyway? We have to call you something."
I asked as I poured my coffee.
"I... don't know. Do you know?" She asked Flynn.
"No, sweetness, I sure don't."
"So why are you acting so nice to me if you don't know me?"
"Yeah, Flynn, why is that?"
He looked at me like he had just thought of something interesting. I tilted my head and smiled at him while he processed that bit of information.
"You remind me of my little sister, sweetness,

that's all." Then he smiled back at me, and I just turned and mosied into the kitchen.

"Morning Sarah, how you are this fine morning?" I asked as I peeked into the frying pan.

She was sitting at the kitchen table stirring a cup with a slogan that read, "Dough is all you need." I sat across from her. "I think we should call the new girl "Sissy."

"Really? Why?"

"Flynn just told her she reminds him of his sister."

"He isn't acting very brotherly."

"My thought exactly, hence the name."

"I swear, JD, sometimes you confound me."

"I don't know why. I'm about the most sensible person I know".

We laughed when Mason walked in with his coffee; the kitchen had just become popular. Oh, yeah, never mind.

"What's up in here?" he sat at the table. I frowned at him, but he ignored me. Sarah got up to tend breakfast, and Mandy strolled in, all sad. She walked over and leaned her head against Mason's shoulder, and he put his arm around her.

"What's the matter, munchkin?"

"Bubba doesn't like me anymore. He likes that new girl more than me."

Oops!

"Mandy, remember when that mean snake bit your foot and you were sick for a while? Bubba stayed with you just like he's staying with her. He'll be your best friend again as soon as she's well. Till, then, will I do?"

She settled on his lap and giggled, "Oh Mason, you're too big to chase balls."

"Really?"

"Come on, Mandy; eat your breakfast before it gets cold," Sarah said as she placed a plate of scrambled eggs on the table. Mandy kissed Mason's cheek and slipped into the booth to eat. He looked at me and thought, *What?*

I shook my head at him. "Why don't we check the fence line today for more trespassers?"

"As soon as you're ready, meet me on the snowmobile."

"Not till you both get something to eat," Sarah said as she put two plates with deer steak, fried potatoes (from the can), and eggs. Two glasses and a jug of orange juice followed. We forgot the kids in the dining room while we finished our breakfast, then a loud *Fuck!* popped into my mind from Lacy. From the way Mason jumped, he got it too.

A few seconds later, a furious Lacy stomped into the kitchen. She stopped short when she saw us and then tried to decide which way to go.
"Don't even think about it," I said, patting the chair beside me. She looked at Mason, who drank the last of his orange juice and grabbed his coat before going out the back door.
I waited for her to talk. She sat there, hitting the table leg with her foot. I motioned her to follow me upstairs after putting my plate in the sink, then let her stew while I put on the "purple monstrosity' everyone called my snowmobile suit. She paced like a mad woman until I finished.
"Make it quick, or I'll melt in this thing."
"Randy thinks the new girl is sweet. Randy thinks the new girl should have some of MY clothes since she doesn't have any. Randy thinks that my new coat would fit the new girl better. Randy thinks..."
"Okay, I get the picture. Where is Randy right now?"
"Randy is getting the new girl her breakfast or trying to without tripping over Flynn or his own big, damned feet. What the hell do those two see in her?"
"Flynn said she reminds him of his sister."

"Then he must be into incest because that boy does not have brotherly thoughts about her. And Randy....!"

"Okay, okay, we've already been over that. Look, there is nothing you can do, and it will worsen if you make a big deal about it. Give the novelty of a new person in the group a chance to wear off. Can you do that?"

"Yeah, but she ain't getting any more of my clothes. I have to put my foot down, and it's down, and he better get over it. Thanks for listening, sis," she said, then kissed my cheek and hurried from the room. Just. Like. That.

I shook my head all the way down the stairs and told Sarah what we would be doing as I put my boots on and stepped out into the fresh, clean air. Mason sat on the snowmobile waiting for me, checking the area with binoculars. When I came down the stairs and walked toward him, he smiled big, and I thought about the new girl causing all this trouble. Maybe the next few months would be hell, and perhaps we might become a great big family, but either way, I had a way to escape when things got bad. He was sitting on it right in front of me.

CHAPTER 13

It was Sunday, which meant pork chops, applesauce, and chocolate cake. The cake was cooling on the counter. I finished the dishes from breakfast while watching Mandy and Bubba chase a chicken in the yard. Barking and squealing mixed with the squawking of the chicken and feathers flying everywhere made it an entertaining show. Sarah and I would go into hysterics every once in a while, watching them play.
Lacy and Randy were still on shaky ground, but only because Sissy encouraged him. She'd managed to piss off nearly all of us in ten days, including Howard, who had treated her like a daughter. Her memory was still AWOL, and she used it to her advantage. She avoided, screwed up, or pitied someone into doing every chore we'd asked of her.
How can you do a load of laundry and everything come out blue, or every egg gathered broken, and

potatoes scorched? We've found her asleep during monitor watch once and watching TV the next time. She'd shrug it off with a whiny "sorry" or collapse in a torrent of tears till either Flynn or Howard or Randy would feel sorry for her. Randy was starting to see the light, and Lacy was noticing. Flynn was giving her odd looks, and Howard had scolded her twice.

 didn't know how much longer she would be able to skate by, but I was positive it would last as long as she could make it. I waited as long as I could before giving the speech, and I knew no one else would do it, so I saved it up.

I was draining the green beans and watching the kids play when Flynn walked up and chuckled at them too.

"Tell me, JD, honestly, what do you think of Sissy?"

"You know me to tell it any other way, Flynn?" I said as I set the colander on a paper towel and proceeded to dry my hands. "She's trouble: lazy, irresponsible, and probably dangerous in the right situation. I don't know how much memory she has because I don't trust her, but I know she's argumentative and loves to instigate fights. A case in point is Randy and Lacy."

Don't hold anything back, JD. Tell me how you really feel."

"I feel like there's going to come to a point when she's going to have to decide where she wants to live. Here or out there somewhere. We have strife around here because of her, and after all, we've been through, we don't need that." I touched his cheek, and he leaned into it. "You must decide just how much you want her to be the sister you lost and if you can stand to lose her again."

Well, now ain't this sweet," said a sarcastic Mason."

Fuck off, meathead," Flynn said. Then he said, "You do what you must to keep this place running right. I trust you to make the right decisions." Then he kissed my palm and walked out to watch the kids.

Mason walked over and looked out the window. I picked up the camera and started retaking pictures. Mandy and Bubba sat on the top step, and she was talking to him. I opened the window a bit, feeling the cool air brush past my hair. "It won't be long now. Bubba. Santa is gonna come off the top of that highest mountain over there," and she pointed at the mountain. He looked at it too. Click! ..." and he is gonna bring us all kinds of presents. That means gifts." She pets him as he gazes lovingly up at her. Click! Click! "Then on Christmas morning, real early, and I know how you hate to get up early, but it's just one day out of the year, ya know, so you can do it, and tear open the presents and find out what Santa brought us." Bubba looked at her and sighed. Then she picked him up and hugged the stuffing out of him. Click! Click!

I shut the window and turned to Mason, who was still watching them.

"That's the reason we have to do something about Sissy. She was what I was discussing with Flynn when you so rudely interrupted."

"Well, it looked like you were getting ready to get dirty." If I decided to 'get dirty with a duck, it's none of your business, Mason. Just keep that in mind for future reference." I turned to leave, and he stopped me with a soft "Wait."

I waited.

"I'm sorry. Okay? When I see you with Flynn, I go crazy. I can't help it. I care about you. Please, forget I said anything."

"No problem. Would you tell Sarah and Lacy they can come back into the kitchen now? They have been eavesdropping for quite a while now."

The persons in question walked boldly into the kitchen like they hadn't heard a word. "I don't know what you're talking about," Lacy said as she got a pot out for the green beans. Sarah just smiled and winked at me.
"I rest my case."
Later, road rash," he said with a wink.
Ass," I mumbled under my breath.
I heard a loud "I heard that from the dining room."I stuck my tongue out at him.
"That's mature ."Said Lacy.
I think I'd spank Mandy's butt for that behavior," Sarah said and then laughed.
The rest the afternoon bumped right along nicely. The next day, however, went to hell fast. We sat around the fire talking about our favorite vacation places when screams echoed throughout the lodge. We found Lacy and Sissy in a full-blown fight with torn clothes and bloody noses. After pulling them apart and calming them down, the reason for the fight slowly came to light.
Take it off," Lacy demanded. "it isn't yours. Take it off.!"
You weren't wearing it," yelled Sissy. "What do you care?"
Wait a minute. Take what off?" I asked.

That blouse she's wearing, mom got it for me before she went to Italy last year. She didn't even ask." Now the excitement was over, Lacy was in tears, and Randy came up and put his arm around her cuddling her close.

"Oh, now she's gonna use tears to get it back. Well, fine, you want it bitch, here." A loud ripping sound brought all eyes back to Sissy as she tore the thin material off her. Then she threw it at Lacy, and after making sure everyone saw her bare breasts, turned and stomped back to the clinic, slamming the door.

Lacy grabbed the blouse from the floor and ran to her and Randy's room. Howard turned and slowly walked outside, head hanging low. Mason, Flynn, Duke, Sarah, and I just stood there with our mouths hanging open.

Well. Hell." Flynn said.

Yeah," Duke agreed, then turned and returned to the monitors. I took a deep breath and decided whether I should console Lacy or knock the shit out of Sissy. I turned and walked into the dining room instead, got a plate and fork, and cut a piece of coconut cream pie. Sitting at the table nibbling on the pie, the others slowly came in and milled around the room. Mason stood at the window and looked at nothing, Flynn held the door jam up, and Sarah sat opposite me.

"We have to do something soon," Sarah said.

"'Yeah, I know." I looked at each of them in turn. "Who wants to be the bad guy here?" No one said a word. "Oh, why does it always have to be me?"

"You can say what needs to be said and mean it. The rest of us are too easygoing." I looked at Flynn, and he straightened up fast. "Not that you aren't easy going, JD, so take that look off your face. It's just that we tend to give in, and you stand your ground."

"Is everyone prepared to stand behind me no matter what I say? Cause I may have to be mean, and I want everyone to back me up."

"Something has to be done, and now is as good a time as any. I'll back you up no matter what you say or do. I always have your back, no matter how wrong you are." I looked sharply at Mason, ready to cuss him out, when I saw the smile.

"Remember what a hard ass I am, Mason, and we'll get along just fine. Soon as I finish my pie, I'll talk to her, and I'll need a witness. Sarah, would you do the honors?" She nodded, then we became quiet while I figured out what I would say.

I finished my pie, sighed heavily, looked at everyone, and got up. As I walked by, Flynn clapped me on the back, and Mason winked. I would have rather been tortured by aliens than do what I had to do now. But some things can't be helped, and I was a hardass.

was standing at the door to the clinic when Howard walked in. He looked at me and said, "Do what you have to. I'm ashamed I brought her here to hurt the Lacy girl like that and then to display herself on top of it. I wash my hands of her." I walked over to him and hugged him. He patted me on the back and then headed to the kitchen. I took a breath and opened the door to the clinic. Something bounced off the wall two feet from my head and crashed to the floor. It was a vase. I looked down at it, then at Sissy, and closed the door. I pulled the stool out, sat, and spun around in slow circles waiting for Sarah to come in. "Well, you gonna say anything or just sit on your fat ass ."I turned back and forth on the stool, watching her as she sat on the bed and watched me. Her arms were folded under her breasts which had been covered with a gray tee shirt. She leaned against the headboard, waiting for me to say or do something. Sarah came in, closed the door, and leaned against it, quietly watching.

"Well, don't knock or anything. Just barge right in. You stuck-up bitches are all alike."

Sarah's brows went up into her hairline then she glanced at me.

"You have given up all right to civilized behavior after that display earlier. You have given up the right to do anything around here, including live."

"That bitch..."

"...is my sister, and I love her dearly." I started to pace. She'd finally pissed me off. She shrank back against the headboard. Good, she was finally scared of me.

"That blouse was a gift from our mother on a shopping trip they took before our parents went on a second honeymoon to Italy. They died in a plane crash on the return trip. Now that is the last explanation you're getting from me. You're useless—a boil on a society fighting tooth and nail to exist. When I see something like you, I usually kill it". Her eyes were getting bigger and bigger.

"Anyway, I think in your case, Sissy, or whatever your name is, it's time for you to find another place to..." waving my hands wildly, "...whatever. We saved your life, bitch, we can take it away".

"Wait. You can't do that, and you can't make me leave. The guys won't let you." She was so sure of herself—what a shame.

"Do you see them here defending your honor, poor as it is?"

"They..."

"Shut. Up." She did.

"Hard times call for hard measures, so this will happen. You will be given one week to kiss enough ass to convince everyone, and I do mean everyone, of your sincere intentions to become a productive member of this lodge. If one person has doubts at the end of that week, you will be returned to the roadhouse in the clothes you have on your back and one week's provisions. A militia group about 50 miles west of here is short on women and would LOVE to have you around." I stood up and turned towards the door, then turned back.

"Oh yeah, if you decide to leave now, I'm sure one of the "guys" will be more than happy to take you back to the roadhouse cause they've had enough of your crap too. But be very sure of this. I will not tolerate one more moment of your bullshit."

By now, I had both hands on the bed and was leaning forward halfway across it. I made eye contact because I wanted to be sure she understood every word I said. "I was all for putting a bullet in your brain and feeding you to the hogs, and the consensus was that it wasn't civilized. But push me, please, push me, and no one on this planet will be able to stop me. Clean up this mess you made, and before I forget, we start fixing supper around five, be there ready to help, or be ready to leave."

Sarah said Sissy sat on that bed with her mouth hanging open and a glazed look in her eyes. I didn't care; I felt like I'd been pushed into it and wasn't happy with anyone. I went up to Lacy's room and started to knock when I heard the unmistakable sounds of lovemaking. Doing a quick turn-about, I went to my room, shutting the world out. I lay on the bed, stared at the ceiling, and soon fell asleep.

Two hours later, I was in the kitchen with my head stuck in the fridge. I don't know what I was looking for but was sure I would know when I found it. Grabbing a piece of Sarah's homemade bread, I put a heaping tablespoon of peanut butter on it and sat at the table with a glass of water. Mason popped into my head. How *ya doing, short stuff?*

Just fine, gut face, how are you?
am just coming back from the fence line. It's looking good. Want to go on a ride with me little girl? I grinned and worked the wad of peanut butter with my tongue from the back of my throat. *No, it's almost time to start dinner, and I want to see what Sissy's doing. Maybe later. Okay, I'll be in in a few minutes to see the show. It looks like snow is coming in, so I want to put in some wood.*

heard the snowmobile in the distance. Flynn came in and dug around in the fridge for a few minutes. He looked at what I had, shuddered, and attacked the cupboards. I looked at the clock, then out the window, and it was getting darker sooner, and I hated that.

"I've been watching a flock of turkeys in the next valley. Been thinking about going hunting in a few days. What with Thanksgiving coming on, thought it would be nice to have a big turkey in the oven."

"Hmmm, that sounds wonderful. I know we have a ham we could eat that day, but I was counting on a turkey."

"That must be Mason coming back. I wish he wouldn't go out alone like that, but we're sort of safe right now, so I guess it's alright".

"In that case, maybe you should take him hunting when you go out. I'd feel better if you buddy up." He smiled at me, and I just shook my head. These guys misunderstood me on purpose to see me blush. Not today, I was still wound up, and waiting for five o'clock to come was getting on my nerves. I heard voices from the other room and then a door shut, so I moved into the dining room.

I nodded at Howard, then Flynn came in, and Sarah with Mandy in tow, and Bubba followed. Mason came in the back door, took off his hat, coat, and boots, then fixed himself a cup of coffee and sat with the rest of us. Five o'clock came, then at two minutes after, a door closed in the front of the house, and a dressed Sissy walked slowly into the dining room.

Randy and Lacy stood behind her as she slowly walked into the room. She looked at me with pure hatred and then turned to the others.

I want to say that I'm sorry for what an ass I've been." She waited for someone to jump in and contradict her. When no one did, she sighed and continued. "I blamed you all for my problems, the virus, hell, for just about everything. I was so

miserable that I had to fend for myself, not knowing how and doing fairly bad at it, that I took it out on all of you. I'm going to try to do better. Really. Cause JD said she'd put a bullet in my brain and feed me to the hogs if I don't, and I don't figure getting ate by hogs is any better than getting eaten by walkers, so, well anyway, I'm going to try to do better and make my life easier and you all's life better in the process."
Everyone had problems keeping a straight face; Howard had to cough a few times. Lacy and Randy didn't say anything; Lacy went to the kitchen, so Sarah, me, and Sissy followed. She stood around, uncertain what to do, so I picked out several cans of food and set them on the counter, pointed to the manual can opener, and supervised for several minutes. I wondered if she would say anything about the electric can opener right in front of her, but she was smart for once, or maybe she didn't recognize one.
Dinner was nice for once also—a friendly, quiet good-for-the-digestion affair.

CHAPTER 14

Mason was right about snow coming in. It came down for two whole days, and then it got cold. The highs in the single digits cold. The kind of cold where you can't tell the difference between zero and minus or plus ten degrees. It was just plain cold. The 40-mile-an-hour winds didn't help, but the wind in Montana was natural. We tried to ignore it, but the sound of it howling and the snow swirling and dancing outside the windows made the cozy fire just that much nicer.

We had the big fireplace roaring, and Sissy was busy carrying in wood several times a day. Her idea, not ours. Randy had scooped out a path to the livestock pens, but other than that, we hunkered down to wait for the warm snap that usually visited Montana in fall.

Flynn disappeared two days before Thanksgiving and came in later with two glorious birds. Cleaning them turned into an exciting endeavor, but we somehow tucked the cleaned birds into the bottom of the fridge until they could go into the oven.

We were all involved in keeping Mandy busy. Duke tried to play hide and seek with her, but Bubba kept giving her location away. We planned treasure hunts and put on costumed teas that Sarah and Sissy made themselves. Flynn charmed everyone when he put on a top hat he'd found and drank raspberry tea all day from a tiny cup. He had won her over forever when he bowed to her and seated her at the table. Sissy had written a play with Mandy as Pocahontas and Duke as John Smith, but we had to wait till Thanksgiving Day to see it. We were looking forward to it.

Sissy had turned into a different person, but no one trusted it to last long. She'd improved in the kitchen, and Sarah was busy teaching her to cook, although she still burned the potatoes. I couldn't figure it out, but the closest I could come was she was just not too attentive. Still, she used a timer and everything. Who knows? She had been relegated to the baker position, which she seemed to enjoy, so she planned the desserts for Thanksgiving.

I think Lacy was holding out on approving her because she hated the girl, but I had a way to keep the good behavior coming long after the probation period. I didn't blame Lacy, but I couldn't condemn the girl to death because Lacy was jealous.

Sissy avoided me like the plague. I think she might have been frightened of me, which was good. Mason enjoyed teasing her, and I let him because I still felt mean from having to act mean. Know your enemy and all that. Don't get me wrong, I was nice to her, but I didn't go out of my way to search her out. This is primarily because I was the one to make her take a good long look at herself; she didn't like what she saw, so of course, it was my fault. Just human nature, so no fault there.

Howard came in later that day, shaking his head. "Know that ravine you found all the walkers in? Well, it's full again, but they are frozen stiff. The damnest thing I ever saw, I'll tell you that. Duke made me carry a danged phone so that I could take pictures. But he'll have to take them off. I'll just put the snowmobile up."

We all stood around waiting for the pictures to appear on the monitor. When they did, all we could do was stare. They looked like, well, big mushroom heads planted in the snow. They all had a bluish tint to them, except for a couple that

was just bumps in the snow, but there were seven of them, I could see.
"Well," I said, tilting my head to one side. The damnest thing I ever saw too.
"Yeah," Duke muttered, peering closer at the screen like it would change anything.
"Well," I said again, with an English degree and everything.
Like we were all hooked to see the same string, we leaned toward the monitors, then jumped like we'd been shot when Mandy screamed "Smurfs!!!" pointing at the monitor. "Look, mama, smurfs! Can I have one? Please. I always wanted one. They're famous, you know?" Well, she was right about that. We all looked at Sarah, who looked around at us, her mouth hanging open. "Can I, mom? Please". She was hopping up and down. She was so excited, holding her hands in prayer mode, pleading with big Mandy eyes. Then Sarah seemed to wake up, grabbed Mandy by the hand, and before dragging her from the room, turned back at Duke and said, "Fix this." Then she was gone, but you could still hear Mandy begging until her voice faded away.
We still stood there watching the door. Then we slowly turned and looked at Duke, who wore the

"deer in the headlight look." He looked at us, then back at the monitor.

"I'm screwed," he sighed, putting his head down on his folded arms.

That's all it took. I laughed until I cried. We were in various stages of hysteria. Mason was on the floor. Howard sat in a chair, bent over his knees, laughing himself silly. We laughed for a few minutes, with Duke glaring at us, which made it worse. I couldn't look at the monitor with the planted "smurfs," some budding, some blooming, and some just breaking through the surface. Ok, enough of that.

When everyone finally settled down, we once again stared at the monitor.

"Well, for heaven's sake, they can't be moved till it thaws a bit, then we can kill them."

"Aren't they dead? They're frozen, so doesn't that mean they're dead?' Sissy asked, clearly as puzzled as the rest of us.

"They're probably just frozen. As soon as walkers thaw, they'll re-animate or whatever you call it, and we'll have to kill them anyway. We might as well do it before they wake up. Or whatever you call it. Maybe next week. Any ideas? Anyone?"

Some just shook their heads, and others shrugged

their shoulders.
I looked once more at the garden of smurfs, then left the room scratching my head and wandered into the dining room. I met Mandy as she ran past me crying, headed for Duke, no doubt. She'd work on him till he yelled at her, then she'll grab Bubba and cry herself to sleep. Poor dog.
Mandy bulled till Thanksgiving, then got excited cause she was 'gonna be a star in a play.'
Everything was hush, but it was hard to miss her excitement. The lodge smelled like Thanksgiving with turkey and pies, while cinnamon hung thick in the air.
Mason had checked the smurf garden and decided they could wait for a few days. It bothered me, but not too much could be done since it was too cold and the snow too deep. It could wait, but I didn't have to like it. Maybe it had just been a while since I'd killed anything, and I was feeling it—bloodthirsty ole me.
Lacy and I were setting the table when the alarm went off. Lacy dropped a glass, and I nearly wet myself. Not sure what the noise was, I just stood there, trying to figure it out, when Lacy said "Come on" and took off for Dukes Den. As soon as she said that, I knew it was the security alarm.

Everyone met in the great room.

"Helicopter," Duke pointed, "from the north." We heard the rotors then, looked out, and a military helicopter was hovering in the parking area.

"Attention lodge," we jumped when the walkie Duke was holding went off. He juggled it a moment before holding it at arm's length for all to hear.

"Request permission to land ."I nodded and motioned for Duke to respond. He shook his head and offered the walkie to me. Mason took it and said, "Permission granted" then, he said, "They have bigger guns, and they didn't have to ask." I agreed.

I let down my mental walls and read three confused minds in the chopper. Anticipation, fear, and hope washed over me in waves. I struggled to replace my walls and looked at Mason, who smiled at me.

Flynn was already putting on a coat and gloves, so we joined them. "Might be a good idea if your arm yourself with small guns until we know for sure. We have a pretty good idea they're friendly, but best to side with caution right now. I know how badly you want to greet them, JD, but it might be best if you stand back and watch instead."

I know they wouldn't like the idea of a female deciding she was better than them and running the place. So go, I'm not mad.

You're so special, he said, making a silly face.

You're such an ass. Go, oh mighty zombie slayer, go and impress the masses.

"Good grief," Lacy mumbled.

I turned to her and crossed my eyes, and tilted my head.

She shook her head and smiled.

They met an older soldier who was followed by a younger one. One remained in the helicopter, which was a smart move. All shook hands, and then they came inside.

"Everyone, I'd like to introduce Major Jacobs and Sargent Blair of the Montana National Guard." Mason introduced everyone to the two men.

"Excuse me, Major, we were just sitting down to Thanksgiving dinner, and we'd be honored if you and your men would join us."

Now that we were closer, I could feel waves of pain radiating from the major. He was hurt, but I couldn't fathom where.

"Ma'am, I can't imagine anything I would like

more in the world. It smells like home in here, don't you agree, Blair?"

"Yes, sir, just like home."

So we all turned and went into the dining room, where we jockeyed chairs and tables. Blair would eat and then go out and relieve the other man, and Randy would soon relieve Duke, so it all worked out. Mandy said grace, which was amusing since she included the request for a 'smurf' of her own. The major looked at me questionably, and I explained the smurf garden in the ravine, and he found it just as amusing as we did. Dinner was wonderful, with the Major and Blair filling us in on their living conditions. It soon became apparent what the reason for the visit was. There were eight of them altogether, with one married couple. Everyone had gone home when the virus hit but slowly returned when they had nowhere else to go. It had been five months since the last one returned, and they feared there would be no more.

After dinner, we sat around the table enjoying coffee and dessert. Blair had replaced Private Christman in the chopper, and he was busy wooing Sissy, much to her delight. Even the Major was enjoying the show.

"It's time to explain the reason for this visit. Beforehand I'd like to explain our living conditions. We have the top floor of a clothing store blocked off for our use. The walkers have tried numerous times to break in, but we have barely managed to hold our ground. This morning we were attacked, and we lost two people. We can't keep this up. We're outnumbered and tired and running low on ammo. It seems like every place we go, and we get overrun. I think it's the helicopter since they seem drawn to the noise, but I can't help that. We need it. It's kept on the roof of the building next door along with arms and fuel. Winter's been hard on all of us, as heating has become a problem, and now we have an expecting member."

"You're looking for a home, and I understand that, but Major, we aren't a military unit, nor do we want to be. I won't put these wonderful human beings under the rule of the military who haven't done a decent job of protecting us in the past. No offense intended, Major, but we're doing fine on our own. We are a group of citizens trying to survive. I can understand your position, we've all been in something similar, but if your people move in here, they will be civilians, nothing else."

"YOU won't allow it. I thought Mr. Mason, here was the leader of this group."

Mason shook his head. "No, sir, I'm sorry if I gave that impression, but we're a democratic society here. No one is a leader of this group, although JD is the one who led us here. We all decide what is best for us, and we wouldn't let you or anyone else do that for us."

"Major Jacobs, the last person that wanted to lead us, was shot in the head and fed to the hogs." He thought about it for a minute, sipping his coffee. "We became people trying to survive the moment that virus popped up. I have one hot head, but I would prefer you didn't feed him to the hogs, which might give them indigestion. To counter him is our medic, who is a wonder with a great disposition." That brought smiles all around.

"There'll be seven new people. Can you accommodate that many?"

"I thought you said eight," asked Duke.

He didn't say anything, and I finally figured out why.

"Major, when were you bitten?" I said softly.

The tension level soared through the roof. Everyone sat up straighter. Even Private Christman became more attentive.

Major Jacobs' smiled, "You're very observant, JD. I don't think my men knew that much."

"No, sir, we didn't. I'm sorry, sir".

"Bullshit, Private, you all know what you have to do, and I'm sure you'll do it. It will be the last order I give and the last one you have to obey. I'll be with my Bonny soon, and I'm looking forward to it. I won't be returning with my people, JD. That's why I'd like to know they have a home where they'll be safer than I've been able to make them."

"Well, sir, we'll have to take a vote, so if you'll excuse us..."

"I don't need to talk about it, JD," said Sarah, "I vote, yes."

"Me too, JD, there's room. I vote yes to." Lacy said with tears in her eyes.

It was unanimous. After we packed up some of the leftovers to send with them, we said goodbye and then set about making rooms ready for the newcomers.

We had to take time out for the play, though. Mandy had worked too hard and been too excited to forego it, no matter the reason. It was hilarious, and Sissy was commended for the direction, with Mandy receiving an "Oscar," a cowboy statue on a horse sitting on my bedside table. Duke was great as John Smith, although his hat was almost bigger than he was, and he kept tripping over his boots.

I was trying not to mourn the Major since I'd just met him, but he was heavy on my mind when the helicopter returned later that evening. We directed it to land in the back while we sent out snowmobiles to receive the guests. The major was not with them; a solemn group came in, tired, sad, and bearing gifts. It was good that they had lived above a clothing store because they all had new clothes except one. I figured him to be our hard case as he stomped around and gave orders. The others seemed frightened of him, and I think he liked it that way.

Lacy and Randy had made up the other honeymoon suite for the married couple. She was about seven months pregnant, and the sitting room would make a great nursery. The other female, whose name was Sandy, was put in the room adjoining mine. The rest of the men found spaces in the basement.

We found out later that the major died about three hours after he left us. An hour after he died, he awoke as a zombie and was put down. They had brought his body back, which I didn't like, and we had him stored in one of the caves. Come spring, we'd bury him somewhere lovely on the north forty, with full military honors, whatever that meant.

The newbies slept in the next day. I don't know if it was weariness or if they felt safe for the first time in nearly a year. They started filtering into the dining room around 10 am. Apologetically, they got their coffee and, after some encouragement, brought their breakfast in warming trays on the buffet. They were a quiet bunch that first day, but we quickly figured out the hothead.

He stomped into the room and plopped down in a chair. At the head of the table and glared at the rest of us. Looking at Sandy, he ordered coffee. I got up, grabbed his mug, filled it, and slammed it down in front of him, splashing coffee all over us. He started to jump up when I grabbed his shoulder, pressing on the nerve there. He froze, obviously in pain. I leaned on him till I was near his ear.

"That is the last time you will be served in this lodge. You are just another flunky like the rest of us. If you can't live with that, you will be thrown out. Any questions?"

He glared at me until I stepped back. He looked at the rest of us, and we all just smiled back at him.

"We are an elite military unit..."

"Were," said Flynn

He looked at Flynn, wanting to do something else so badly he nearly vibrated with it.

"I am commander..."

"Were."

"The major is dead, and I'm next in line of the chain of command. That makes me the new commander."

"This ain't a military compound; you ain't any major or commander of nothin. You gonna cause trouble you leave, now." Wow, that Howard sure could talk. "You think you can be a contributor around here, you're welcome, but no one waits on you or takes orders from you. End of story."

"Look... what's your name?" I thought I'd better say something before this got out of hand.

"Major Calvin Sweets."

"Look, Sweets, we would love to have you here if you can follow the standard rules of civilization. No one runs this place, and we all have a say in what happens here, like one big happy family. We had a stupid ass, and I'm not implying you're stupid, who wanted to be the boss. We ended up killing him to have any peace. We don't want to have to do that to do you, but we'll do what we must to survive. So, give us trouble, and we bury you with the major next spring."

He looked at his ex-military soldiers, who wouldn't look at him. They just sat, ate their breakfast, and drank their coffee like we were discussing the weather. He slowly got up, gave them each a glare, and said, "If any of you agree with these *people*, then you will be committing treason, and in a court of law, that is a death sentence."

Private Blain, or just Blain now, looked at him and said, "What part of what they said don't you understand? Even the Major told you the military was done. The government was done, and the law was nonexistent. None of us are part of anything except life, and these nice people are decent enough to bring us into their home. We appreciate it, but you can't grasp that you will never be anything more than a stupid ass, embarrassing yourself in front of strangers who only want to help you." His voice had started to get louder and louder. "I won't let you ruin this for the rest of us. You have done nothing but cause trouble since the moment you arrived, and I, for one, am sick of it. You cause one bit of trouble, Calvin, and I will be happy to smother you in your sleep."

The others stood at that and backed him up. Calvin backed up a step, and when he realized he had, he stepped forward again, but it was too late.

"You can't do this."

"Consider it done."

He looked at everyone in turn and then left the dining room. A sigh of relief was heard, and then everyone started talking. Someone told a joke, and we laughed, but I wondered in the back of my mind how soon old Calvin would show his ass. I wouldn't have to wait long.

CHAPTER 15

I was hanging Christmas garlands over the fireplace mantle when I felt a familiar tug on my pants. "Hold on a sec, Mandy, I just need to get this ..."

"Where's Sweetie going with the toper?" she asked. Sweetie was her name for Calvin Sweets, our resident pain in the ass.

"Hmm?" I mumbled, reaching to loop the garland over a hook.

"Sweetie?"

"What about him?"

"He took the toper by himself, and you said we can't go anywhere alone. Dad said it too, so he's in trouble, right JD?"

I froze and yelled, "Duke! Mason! Flynn! Joe!" and jumped from the ladder. Running into the Duke's Den, I found him unconscious behind a chair and dark monitors. "Medic!" I yelled, moving the chair aside and feeling for a pulse. He moaned then and tried to sit up. There was a deep cut above his eye, so I pressed my hand over it to staunch some of the blood. Joe, our new medic, ran in and began to examine him. I could hear the sound of helicopter rotors pounding outside the lodge.

While Sarah and Joe helped Duke to the clinic, I ran to the door and looked out. Mason, Flynn, and Randy were busy putting on coats while I watched the helicopter approach the front of the building. Lacy and Melody raced up to give them their rifles.

"That isn't good," I whispered. The boys stepped onto the porch as the helicopter hovered before them, sending dirt and snow everywhere. Calvin tried to operate some control and was frustrated at not getting a response. He gave us the finger and turned the copter to the side, racing towards the 'smurf garden.'

Suddenly, it spits, sputtered, and began to spin. Veering sharply to one side, the tips of the rotors almost touching the ground, it dropped into the ravine with a thunderous crash, throwing up snow, rocks, and debris. The noise seemed to last forever, then suddenly it got quiet.

We were in shock. My mind couldn't comprehend

what my eyes and ears had just experienced. Duke popped into my mind the same time Mason did. *Check on Duke for me, would you? I'll check on this idiot, and he better be dead, or I'm going to kill him.*
Kill him once for me, will you?
I found a drowsy Duke trying to get off the exam table while Joe hovered nearby with a hypodermic so he could stitch Duke's head. Duke kept pushing him away while Sarah tried to talk to him. Joe finally gave up, prepared another needle, and injected Duke when he wasn't looking. Soon a sleepy Duke was mumbling about his babies, which meant his computers, while Joe stitched his cut. Lacy brought Mandy in, who immediately crawled onto the table with Duke and started telling him the story of the 'toper.
"He'll want to sleep, but I'd rather he didn't for a while. That was a nice knock on the head he got. I wouldn't have had to sedate him if he hadn't been fighting me. Mandy can keep him awake, I'm sure."
"We'll take care of everything. Sarah, you stay with Duke." Samantha, the new mechanic, said. Sarah smiled her thanks and sat beside the table, gazing lovingly at him.

Duke's gonna be ok. I thought to Mason. *Have you found that bastard yet?*
The copter is totaled, and let me see. Shit!
What?
Damned smurfs scared the crap out of me. I forced my mind to be; still, I would laugh later.
Aw, lookie here, he's still breathing.
Quiet.
Mason?
Oops, I was wrong. Too bad, so sad. And cold. I'm coming back now.
We had another body to dispose of now but not with military honors. I think he would have blown us up, killing everyone, so I did not pity him. I checked on Duke again and then walked into the kitchen to see what the kids were doing. Samantha, or Sam as Howard liked to call her, and a pregnant Melody was busy working on lunch. I wasn't surprised to see Howard sitting at the table. I think he was developing an interest in Sam, and she was closer to his age, and the feelings were mutual. I thought it was cute. I scooted into the booth, forcing Howard to move some. I still have to have my back to the wall. Go figure. Melody brought me a glass of tea.
"How is ya feeling, kiddo?" I asked, sipping the

cool tea. It's funny how we had a life and death situation minutes ago, and the next thing you know, we are chit-chatting and drinking iced tea. That tells you how far from civilization we had come.

"Good. Is it true about Sweets? Is he dead?"

"Yeah, sorry about that, but he brought it on himself. He didn't want to or could not accept his demotion to a human being."

"Please, don't apologize; I'm glad he's gone. He was going to get us all killed eventually with his recklessness. He came close a few times but always blamed it on someone else. It's a relief we don't have to put up with his crap anymore."

Sam came over and sat at Howard's end of the table, making his eyes shine. They spoke low for a few minutes, then Bubba walked over to her and begged to be held. I was a bit surprised about that, but he was an equal opportunity dog and took advantage shamelessly.

Melody said, "Sam and I were talking and wondering about the old greenhouse. I'm a fair gardener, but Sam is better, and we thought if we could find some seeds, we'd like to plant some vegetables. That is if it's ok with everyone else."

"If you are interested in the greenhouse, consider

it yours. It'll need some fixing up, and Duke would have to see how much electricity it would use for the grow lights, but I think, in the long run, it'd be a great asset to our food supply. We'd love some tomatoes in winter and potatoes and lettuce salad." I closed my eyes, "Man, I would just love to graze." I opened my eyes and saw them looking at me. Ok, so much for this. "Go for it," I said and left the room.

I stuck my head in the clinic, and when I saw everything was good, I started to back out when Duke gestured for me to come in.

"You should be resting."

"Bull..." He looked over at the sleeping Mandy..." crap. That so and so took down our security system as soon as these crazy people..."

"Duke," Sarah admonished.

"Well, I need to get the system back up, see if he broke anything, and fix it. I told Mason and Flynne what to do, but unless I..."

"...do it yourself, you aren't gonna trust anyone else to do it right."

"Something like that, yeah," he whined.

Mason came in, sat down, and looked at Duke. "It's all up and running like before, and all he did was disconnect the system. One of the cameras is

snowy, but otherwise, it looks good."
"How can it look good when one of the cameras is down?"
"You can check it out yourself as soon as Joe releases you and not one second before. Do you hear me? You, little jackass. You scared the hell out of me, and I will fight you tooth and nail to do what the doctor says. Now shut up and rest."
We took the hint and left, just short of running out of the room. Hell, she scared me when she got like that, and I know she's mad when she in any way refers to his size. He knew it, too, that's why he shut up.
Mason walked beside me to the dining room, coming so close to holding my hand that I felt the heat from his arm. If he knew how close to jumping his bones I was, he would've run. But I could control myself. Couldn't I?
Joe had been eating lunch with Sissy, and things were looking cozy with them, too, but I sensed his side was offering friendship. What was up? Everyone seemed to be pairing off like we were on the ark or something. Oh, wait, we were, sort of. At the very least, we were insolated. It was winter, cold nights, and all that. I'm going to ignore it. That's what I'm gonna do.

To make sure I could do that, the powers that be sent Flynn into the dining room to sit next to me. That put me in between them. Oh, for heaven's sake.

"Duke just told me he was the one that sabotaged the chopper."

"You're kidding? Is there anything that guy doesn't know?"

"He did something to the stabilizer prop. The stabilizer prop is the small prop at the end of the tail, which keeps the helicopter from spinning like a top. That's why Sweets couldn't control it. He also disconnected the weapons control module. Remember when he hovered in front of the porch? He was trying to shoot a missile at us. When it didn't work, he shot us the bird instead. Duke said when he was released from solitary, he'd help scavenge the parts from the copter, don't ask him to help remove the body. His choices of words were rather inventive to describe what he'd do to Sweets if he had survived the crash."

"I bet. Sweets were probably lucky, from the way it sounds. I don't think anyone is gonna miss him."

The ladies brought out lunch, and we ate in silence. Flynn leaned toward me and whispered loud enough for Mason to hear, "I found a crib in the attic, and I thought it would make a great gift for Melody and Dave, for the baby."

I looked at him like he'd grown horns. "Well, aren't you just full of surprises?"

He shrugged and wandered back to the basement. He had some project he was working on, but I had no idea what. It was getting close to Christmas, so I wished him luck. Randy was manning the monitors, and after mind searching for Lacy, I found her in her room, reading a magazine. How many of those things does she have?

I went back to hanging garland again. It seemed like days since I started. So much had happened. It was hard to imagine this was even the same day. I thought of the crib in the attic and decided there was something I could do about personalizing it. I was thinking of baby things while I finished the great room.

I had worked on it non-stop for days, and it looked festive. All we needed was the tree. The guys were going out tomorrow to get the one Lacy, and I had picked out months ago. We'd found some popcorn, tiny lights, and ribbons, which were hiding in the crib, and we planned to show Mandy how to make paper chains for the tree. It was such a normal thing to do we were all looking forward to it.

I grabbed the box of leftover decorations and took it back to the attic. Looking closely at the crib, I decided how to decorate it so it would fit a boy or girl. Mason grabbed me from behind as I turned to leave and nuzzled my neck. I let him. I know, but winter, cold nights, bone jumping, and all that, remember? His arms were folded beneath my tingling breasts. I was in trouble, but I couldn't decide if it was such a bad thing.

My experience with men was short and not so sweet. I had no idea what I had in store. This mind-reading thing wasn't always so controllable. Imagine hearing a man thinking the whole time if he could catch that chick down the hall when he got home. Or gee, I thought her breasts were bigger, or this makes the fourth one this week. I'm the man.

I shouldn't have that problem with Mason because we could talk and kiss at the same time, and man, could he kiss. The soft, deep, toe-curling, hungry for more kind. His nuzzling of my neck was doing things down low, and I decided to do something about it. He started to tug at my shirt.

"Oh, well...maybe..." I couldn't seem to form a coherent thought and nearly lost my mind when his warm hands snuggled under my bra except for his thumbs which had found my nipples through the thin material.

"I've missed you," he said as his teeth tugged gently at my earlobe. The one on the right, yep, that's the one, and it's the most sensitive.

"Where have I been?" I whispered. Moving my bottom against him, I found out just how happy he was to be there.

"Nowhere you should have been. Like with me. Have you missed me?"

"Huh?" I heard a ripping sound as my bra gave way and the cool air of the attic caressed my stomach.

"Shhh," he whispered, turning me toward him. I unbuttoned his shirt briskly and eased it out of his pants and off his shoulders. I unbuckled his belt and began to work on the snap of his jeans. For some reason, my fingers didn't want to work right, and I became desperate.

He took my hands and led them up to his chest. "Slow, cookie, slow," he said, his voice gone all soft and shivery just before his lips claimed mine again. I could feel myself relaxing inch by stubborn inch and began to stroke his chest as he'd stoked mine. His hand went behind my head and

pressed gently, deepening the kiss until I was almost crazy with the desire to get that zipper down. This time it cooperated, and I began to push down his pants. He helped me to lie down on the mattress I'd walked on minutes before. He gazed down at me, touched my cheek, and slowly bent down to kiss me again. That was the beginning of a long, wonderful attic day.
As attics go, that one was the best.
Getting dressed except for my poor bra, we walked down the stairs smiling at Lacy as she came from her room. She stopped, looked at us, and smiled, giving me the thumbs up. I know my face was fire engine red, so I refused to look at Mason. He waltzed softly through my mind, caressing me gently then was gone. I finally looked at him, and his face held the look of a conquering hero. Men!
No one questioned where we'd been. Duke was sitting up eating some soup. Bet that went over well. Plans were made to recover Sweets and get the Christmas tree the next day. It looked like he really was going to be buried with the Major come spring. After all the trouble that idiot had tried to cause, Randy said the compound was secure.
The rich smell of venison stew made my mouth

water as I washed up for supper. I must be hungry.
Go figure.

CHAPTER 16

Mason, Flynne, Randy, and Melody's husband, Dave, left after breakfast to retrieve Sweets' body and get a Christmas tree. Then Duke would dismantle the helicopter and see what he could salvage as soon as he was allowed. Sarah kept a close eye on him, which he complained about, but she ignored him. However, it grated on my nerves.

Sarah had prepared a hearty breakfast for the men and pancakes. After a quick okay, I ignored them for the scrambled eggs and toast. Mandy had her usual hot chocolate and pop tarts. I looked at the chocolate mix, and after a moment's hesitation, I added a packet to my coffee. Not bad.

Later, we were cleaning the kitchen, laughing and kidding around when Mandy said she heard gunshots. We listened and heard nothing, and then we heard a volley of shots.

Mason? Are you guys okay?

No, tell Joe to get ready; we're bringing in Dave. A mountain lion mauled him. It isn't good, JD. I walked quickly towards the clinic and found Howard visiting Duke. "Joe, the guys are bringing Dave in, he's been mauled by a mountain lion." "If you feel okay, Duke, you can go to your room, but rest." Joe said as he grabbed some stuff off the counter, "I'll need some warm water, lots of bandages, and Lacy." Duke scurried off the exam table with Howard's help, then took Lacy's place at the monitors. She prepared the clinic while Joe headed outdoors to wait for the snowmobile fast approaching from the north. As he watched them, he said, "You might want to rally around Melody. We need to keep her as calm as possible."

The girls stood at the window watching the approaching snowmobile but turned when they heard my footsteps. "A mountain lion attacked the guys. I don't know all the details, but Dave," Melody gasped, "was badly injured," she started to the door, but Sam blocked her, "Joe is meeting them on the front porch.

"No," Melody cried, "Not Davey." She pushed Sam out of the way and hurried to the front porch with the rest of us in hot pursuit.

We got to the front door about the same time the

snowmobile stopped at the bottom of the steps. All I could see was a bloody mess of clothes. Melody cried as she followed him inside the clinic, supported by Flynne.
"I need Lacy, Sarah, Randy, everyone else out! That includes you, Mel." She backed up against the wall by the door, crossed her arms over her child, and glared at us. Okay. I pulled a chair over for her, then Flynn helped her sit down.
"You sit right here, and I'll keep you company until Dave wakes up." He stood next to her and put his hand on her shoulder. Lacy and Sarah were busy cutting the bloody clothes away while Joe was doing medic-type things, so I left the room, quietly closing the door. Everyone looked at me, but I could only shrug my shoulders.
"Mason, what happened?"
"When we got to the helicopter, it was surrounded by cat tracks. Big as your hand, those tracks. Sweets left another track as his body was dragged from the helicopter into the woods. Dave wanted to go after him and bring his body back. He said it wasn't right, but we wouldn't do it and started after the Christmas tree. We thought he was behind us, guarding our flank, but when we heard the scream and saw he wasn't back there, we took

off after him. We found him right off, but the cat had already done a lot of damage."

Just then, we heard Melody scream Daves's name and sobs so hard and loud that I grabbed my stomach, "Dammit, dammit, dammit." I sat hard on the ottoman, grief for her loss so heavy I couldn't stand under its weight. I knew what she'd have to go through, and my heart ached for her. Mason rubbed my neck gently as Sam fell into Howard's arms. She'd known him a lot longer than the rest of us. I so did not want to go into that room right then. No way.

A while later, the door opened, and Joe came out. "I've sedated her, although I didn't give her much because of the baby. We have to do something with Dave. She'll need a funeral, now, tomorrow, soon. Get it over with so she can concentrate on that baby. She loses it, and we lose her." He ran his hand through his hair. "Fuck. What the hell kind of fucked up world is this? We were safe. Hell." He sat hard on the chair and continued to ruffle his hair. Taking a big breath, he looked up and said, "At least she won't have to pretend anymore."

Huh? What?

"Sweets was a pain in the ass, but you have no

idea how bad he could get. If he'd known that Dave and Mel weren't married, he would've been all over her whether she wanted him to. It wouldn't have mattered in the least that they were brother and sister. So they acted married to hold Sweets off, although I don't know why that would matter to Sweets. Then there was the little matter of being homophobic. He would've killed Dave if he'd known he was gay. So pretending to be married killed two birds with one stone. They planned to tell everyone today, but it doesn't matter anymore."

"But they've been sharing the same bedroom." Sissy was as confused as the rest of us.

"He's been sleeping on the couch in the sitting room. They'd just found each other after two years, and since they're maternal twins, they didn't look identical. The baby's father died in a plane crash two weeks after she got pregnant."

"JD, there's a cemetery in that town east of here, right on the road...if I remember right, it had a mausoleum. Why don't I run over there and check, maybe make room for Dave? "Randy said.

"Not alone, Randy. No one goes anywhere alone anymore. I'm getting paranoid now. In fact, why don't you take Flynn?"

"Why don't I start planning the funeral, and we take him to one of the cabins until then? They aren't heated, and he would be okay there until the funeral. I don't like the idea of the caves." Lacy had a good idea, and we all agreed to it. The unheated cabin was safe from the animals, and he wouldn't decompose as fast.

Melody, however, became almost catatonic. She just lay there staring into space, not eating or drinking. Joe started an iv to keep her hydrated, but she needed food for herself and the baby. Melody wasn't there right then. Joe was preparing to put in a feeding tube when she finally started to come around.

We'd known we would have to make a run into town in preparation for the baby's arrival, but we thought we had another month or so. It was decided two days after Daves's death. They would check out the funeral homes on the way back. They wanted to find a nice casket for Dave. Lacy was going this time, and although it was her turn, I was still worried. Joe made a list and made sure everyone knew what he wanted.

I don't know how much formula and diapers they could get, but we'd go back to town if we had to. Melody insisted that Dave be buried on the property. She did, however, want a nice casket. Sigh. Okay, well, they would check on it while they were gone. Where and how I had no idea and didn't want to know.

Flynne never left her side as she told us how they had come up with the idea of being married and how Sweets figured into the plan. Only Joe knew about it because he had been Daves's best friend throughout high school. Many people thought they were more than that, but that's how people are. They ignored it and joined the national guard at the same time. Staying close, they managed to be in the same unit, and the friendship continued. He made Flynn understand that Melody was like a sister to him and nothing more, and Flynn just smiled and nodded.

I waved bye to the team the following day, and although I was apprehensive about Lacy going, I tried not to let on. She was so excited that I didn't want to ruin it for her. They had a specific plan, and I was confident it would work cause I knew the team. I just remembered the last time at Walmart.

One thing we had to do while they were gone was getting that damned tree done. Joe let Melody sit on the couch and watch things, but the sadness in her eyes was a distraction. Mandy kept asking her opinion to the point that Joe finally led her back to the clinic where she would live until she had the baby. No more climbing stairs for her. We decorated that tree all day. Mandy would find something else to put on it, and up the ladder, Joe would go. Sissy was at his side to the point he was tripping over her. I finally sent her with Sarah to start supper. She began to object until she remembered our "agreement" and then sulked off behind Sarah while Joe shot me a look of gratitude. When we finally had the tree the way Mandy wanted it, we were too absorbed in Dave's death to be excited.

I was up all night waiting for the crew to return. I paced the floor and wondered what Lacy was doing and if Mason was okay. All night long, I worried and tossed and turned. I couldn't think of a good enough reason for them not to have returned the day before. I cornered Duke the next day and asked if there was something he could come up with that would enable us to communicate at long distances. He said he didn't know but would start working on something. I left him to play with the idea.

I couldn't eat breakfast, so I drank a pot of coffee

instead. Melody was depressed but seemed better that morning. The death of a twin had to be tough, but she handled it the best she could. Dave would have a funeral in the lodge after Christmas, and he would rest in his casket in one of the caves until the ground thawed enough to dig a grave sometime in June. She made all the arrangements, and then she rested. It sounded like a solid plan and one we could all live with.

I sat in the recliner and dozed until Duke yelled the team was back. *Mason, is everyone okay? Yeah, we're okay, just tired. I'll explain when we get in.*

I've been nuts waiting for you to get back. He caressed my mind, then was gone. I ran to the front door at the same time as a caravan of semis and trailers rounded the bend toward the lodge. I had taken to counting them since the time they brought back Flynne, so I was relieved when only three semis pulled to a stop in the parking area. Lacy didn't run to greet me as she would have a year ago, and I missed that hug. They climbed down from the rigs and tiredly shuffled into the lodge. Sarah had thrown together a decent meal, and I was able to wait till dessert before I wanted answers.

"Gee, where to start?" I tried to raise just one eyebrow, but as usual, I just looked surprised. Mason got the hint, and Lacy stifled a giggle. "We didn't have much trouble at the warehouse. There were still several trailers at the dock, so Howard hooked up to one, and I started filling it. I got a lot of baby stuff, formula, diapers, and jars of baby food, though I don't know how good it is yet. I picked up some gardening stuff for the ladies too. We managed to half fill the trailer and then had to find the rest of the stuff."

I refilled his coffee, and he softly kissed my hand. Taking a sip, he continued. "We found several specialty stores in a strip mall on the other side of town, so Howard offered to be the decoy while we mined them." A decoy went as far from the mine area as possible. As soon as the miners were in position, he made some noise. Usually, a car alarm attracts the walkers away from the site. "We broke out the window of a baby store and gave Howard the sign. We heard the alarm and went into the store, bagging and loading as quickly as possible. We were so busy we didn't notice the alarm had stopped until the walkers came barrcling into the store. We didn't know at the time that the car alarm only lasted about five minutes cause the battery ran down."

"I had a hell of a time finding another car with an active alarm, so I used the horn on the truck. By then, Mason and Lacy were locked in a bathroom in the store, and Randy was locked in the trailer." Howard said as he petted Bubba.

We all gasped at that, and then for some reason, I don't know, I got tickled. I could feel the corners of my mouth starting to turn up, and then I laughed. It wasn't funny, but I laugh when I'm tired or nervous.

I remember once in high school. I had this very prim and proper French teacher. She walked around the room, back stiff, smacking a ruler in her hand as we recited french. Anyway, she walked primly and sedately past my desk one day, stepped on a piece of paper, her feet went straight up in the air, and her ass hit the floor. Her hair had come loose from the proper bun she had it in, and a hairpin was dangling from some strands of hair while one shoe had flown three feet away. I was the only one laughing then and the only one laughing now. When I finally got control of myself again, I motioned for Howard to continue while I cleared my throat.

Glancing repeatedly at me, he continued, "So I

drove around blaring my truck horn until I hit a dead end. I mean a dead end, as in the can't-go-another-foot-at-the-cemetery dead end. I'm not real good at backing trailers, especially a 53-foot trailer. So with walkers climbing all over me, I'm trying to back up enough to get turned around. I accidentally hit the truck horn one time, and it stuck. So, unable to go anywhere, I turned the truck off, climbed in the back, and shut the curtains. That horn blared for over an hour before it finally quit, so I figured the battery died."

"Meanwhile," Mason said, "we're in the bathroom with walkers beating on the door. There was a window, but it was one with thick glass blocks you couldn't see through. I knew it would be heard for blocks if I broke it, so we just sat tight."

"I'm in the trailer with walkers bouncing me back and forth like crazy until I finally find something to hang onto," Randy said. "I figured if it were quiet inside, they would eventually disappear. I could barely hear Howard's truck horn, so I didn't know what he was doing."

We all looked at Mason. "We spent most of the night in that bathroom, waiting. We didn't hear anything for over an hour, but I knew they could stand in one place until something got their attention. Truth be known, we were too scared to do anything. I guess Randy was having the same problem. We finally got the walkies to work but couldn't reach Howard.

So now we're all stuck. We managed to doze during the night, but we were so worried about Howard that we didn't sleep well. Anyway, somewhere near dawn, there was a loud explosion. Rocked the building, and Randy said the trailer swayed." Randy nodded his head when everyone looked at him.

"I heard it in my truck's sleeper, so I peeked out the window and saw the walkers headed in that direction. I waited until I couldn't see them, then rolled my window and looked behind me. There was a fireball from hell north of town, so I got out the map and saw a propane company in that area. Not long after the first explosion, I heard trucks racing by a few blocks over and using my binoculars saw they were a bunch of guys wearing scarf things and football helmets." He shrugged his shoulders at that.

I suddenly remembered Del and Dean from the Walmart store a few months back, and they had both worn those scarves on their head. If this was a part of their group, I could almost see them trying to steal propane and screw it up.

"I got out as quietly as possible and disconnected the horn, then tried the battery again. It almost went dead again, but it finally caught. While waiting for the truck to build up air pressure, I looked around and saw a funeral home a block over, and I tried backing up again. I guess I do better when not being chased by a herd of the undead. I pulled up in front of the funeral home and snuck inside, found an empty casket, and using one of those casket hauling carts, and I managed to get one loaded."

"While he's loading caskets, we sneak out, and when we don't see any walkers, get Randy out of the trailer. There isn't a walker in sight, so we raid every store in the mall until Howard drives up as if nothing happened. Smart ass even tipped his hat and said, 'Top of the morning to ya.'"

Howard was grinning about that while holding Bubba, who was licking his cheek. After feeding Bubba some of his leftover steak, he rose. "I'm going to take us for a little walk, then hit the sack. I want to talk to Duke tomorrow about a different communication setup. That was a right fine meal, Sarah. Thank you. Night everyone."

After that, the night got quiet. Sissy and Sarah

cleaned things up while I sat with Randy, Lacy, and Mason. We had three more trailers, and even though one held a casket, that was fine. The others held all kinds of treasure according to them, and I was just glad they were back okay.

Randy and Lacy said their goodnights, went in to visit Melody, and finally climbed the stairs to bed, arm in arm. I walked Mason to his room, where we necked like teenagers till he fell asleep. I went back to my room, showered, and climbed into bed. No one was leaving my sight for the next year. I swear, my nerves wouldn't handle it anymore.

Famous last words.

CHAPTER 17

I put the finishing touches on my lipstick, which looked out of place on me, but it'd been a long time since I went to a funeral. Melody finally figured out how she wanted the funeral and what would be said, so it should be interesting.

I hate funerals. Far as I'm concerned, funerals are for the living, not the dead. I don't want the last image of my loved ones to be of them lying in a casket. Some relatives used to take pictures of the dead in their coffins. Talk about sad. Dave was comfortable in one of the cabins on a bed. At least, that was what I was telling myself. There isn't any heat, so maybe comfortable isn't the right word to use, and he is dead, so he probably doesn't even notice. Who knows, right? Melody does, and that's what matters, but it still gave me the shivers.

I went to the dining room, where everyone was settled at the table eating a light breakfast. I fixed my coffee, feeling everyone's eyes on me. I was still wearing jeans and a tee, but they were black.

It was the best I could do, and I doubted Dave minded. Everyone else looked dressy or as dressy as they could. I sat at the table and sipped my coffee in silence, just managing not to moan at the wonderful taste. The lodge believed in making all its guests as comfortable as possible, so it had invested in the best Columbian coffee. When it ran out, I knew where there was a Starbucks. Mason took my hand, and I smiled at him.
When Melody came in, we all sat upright like we were uncomfortable. It's hard to be comfortable in the face of all that pain. She lumbered to the table where Flynn helped her sit. I wondered about her due date because she looked huge at eight months. I can't be called an expert on that kind of thing, but it made my back hurt to look at her. She smiled her thanks, and his face lit up. When did that happen?
We all rose at the same time, like we were on the same wavelength, and filed into the great room where we solemnly stood in front of the fireplace. Randy had painted a portrait of Dave, which sat on the mantle. Soft music played while Melody spoke of the wonder of her brother and twin. Some of the stories she told were humorous, and some were sad, but she celebrated his life in a

manner that made me jealous. That kind of closeness was unique, and I was honored to see a part of it, no matter how small.

We all spoke of Dave. A few of us who didn't know him well just said a few sentences. Joe spoke of a friendship closer than blood and how losing that friendship would always be felt. I cried with Mason's arm around me. The funeral was over when Melody took down the portrait and silently carried it to the clinic, where she shut the door. Flynn was uncertain about what to do, so I hugged him before going to my room to change clothes.

Mason knocked on my door a few minutes later, and I answered it in my robe. It didn't take him long to remove it and prove to me that life was indeed wonderful. I thought I wouldn't be in the mood, but he changed my mind. As we lay relearning how to breathe, wrapped around each other like a vine, I just felt better.

That was the idea.

The kitchen was busy when I returned a few hours later. I watched the goings on silently as I ate a cinnamon roll and drank orange juice. Everyone was busy, and when someone moved, the other person moved out of the way like it was a dance. I had plans that morning also.

One of the small tables near the corner of the room was laden with arrows, shafts, quivers, points, and the crossbow I was planning to re-string. One of those specialty stores on the strip mall they'd gotten stranded in was an archery store. They brought back cases of arrows and tips. I had a five-gallon bucket of arrows made up, but I like to be prepared, so I'd finish them up. I had several quivers with arrows mounted next to windows on each side of the house. A large bucket was filled with them at each door too. I had a rifle strapped to the door frames with velcro and extra ammo on a handmade shelf next to it. Yeah, I know what you're thinking overkill, right? Well, you never know.

I was also trying to wrap Christmas presents. Some were already under the tree, and I wanted to add my own. Sneaking out to the trailer became a job because someone always tried to follow me. I took my big plastic bag and headed out the door anyway. I was doing a good deed today, so my step was light.

The weather had turned freezing overnight. I pulled the scarf over my mouth and nose, making breathing easier, and tried to unlock the frozen trailer. I set the small lantern on a crate inside and picked out some things I thought everyone would like, pulling the dividing curtain around behind the other stuff so you couldn't see what else was there.

The trailer had been a refrigerated trailer or reefer, so it had sections divided by panels that could be raised and attached to the ceiling when that section was empty. This made it possible to haul frozen items and things like milk and cheese in the same trailer. I was using those panels to hide my gifts from others.

I went back into the kitchen and motioned for Sissy. "Get something warm on. You're going Christmas shopping". She frowned at me but put on her coat and gloves anyway. She tried very hard not to argue with me. I had scared her a while back, and she walked on eggshells around me. I grabbed a knitted cap and slapped it down on her head, and then we went back to the trailer. She oood and aaaaahed for several minutes before she started picking things out.

I told her to take the stuff back to her room, and I'd bring wrapping paper and tape over later.

"Why are you doing this? You didn't have to, you know. It's not like they're giving me anything."

"Well, that's where you're wrong. You're getting something from everyone here, and you want to know why? Because that's the way, we are. We wouldn't for one minute consider hurting your feelings on Christmas day. I didn't want you to feel bad about receiving and not being able to give, so I'm helping you out. I'm not a complete ass." She smiled at me, took the bag, and said, "Your right. You're not a complete ass." I followed her back into the house, smiling. She made a joke. How cute.

I'd brought the gift Lacy had ordered for Randy. Lacy had given me the request before I went to Walmart, and I could find it right off. She already had some paper to wrap, so she grabbed it and shut the door. I knew he was going to love the artist supplies she got him.

I went to Duke's Den to see how he was coming on the communication system. He was working on something in front of the monitors and jumped when I walked in the door. It must be a Christmas gift. Everyone was jumpy, trying to make gifts and get them under the tree. Someone had found a Christmas CD, and music played softly in the background. The smell of pine made it feel like Christmas, and I was in a good mood again.

"I've just about figured out a long-distance communication system, but I still need to test it." I wasn't sure what that entailed, but since no one was going anywhere alone anymore, I'd let the guys figure it out. I wanted to get through December with no one else dying.

Mason walked out of the dining room door about the same time I was entering and grabbed me, kissing the stuffing out of me. "Where you goin?" I asked. He smiled, making my tummy clench. "Now, don't you want to know?" I smiled and playfully punched him in the arm. "Watch it." he said playfully, "I don't play fair." I kissed his nose and smiled. He smacked me on the behind hard enough to sting as he continued past me. *That's, so you know what's coming later*, he thought, and I blushed.

Flynn came out of the clinic, quietly closing the door. "How is she?" I asked. He ran his hand over his bald head and sighed. "I think she'll be okay. It'll just take time. She seems better now that the service is over but still sad, which is to be expected. Joe thinks the baby's okay, so that's good. How are you doing?"

"Better now the service is over. I hate those things mostly because I don't know how to act. If I laugh, is anyone gonna be offended? Am I close enough to the deceased and his family to cry? I don't know. I'm just glad it's over. Mel will be okay because she's strong, resilient, and will bounce back. She needs to do the whole grieving thing. You stay close to her, and she'll be fine."

"I was wondering, in all that stash you've got in that locked trailer out back, you might have something nice I could talk you out of for Melody?"

"I was wondering when you would want to go shopping. You should know everyone here has something for you under the tree. If you want, we can go out later. It's colder than a witch's tit out there, and my feet are frozen, so let me thaw them before I go back out."

"Sure, no problem. I've made several things, but they are big for Christmas Eve, and I want something special for Melody. After lunch is fine. Just holler when you're ready."

Duke yelled for me to come back. He pointed at the monitor, and Randy and Howard dragged something behind them. They'd gone out to check the area where the walker had gotten through before and make it secure. Then they were to bring back the camera that patrolled the gate area.

They were waving wildly and pointing towards the road. So I knew we had company again.
"Hit the siren, Duke...I'll make sure Lacy takes care of Mandy and Bubba." We had practiced it enough, but I was a worried wort and had to make sure. If we invited them in, Sarah's curtains hanging around the doors would hide the armory we'd installed. Checking to make sure everything was in place, I stepped to the door with my shotgun in hand.
The siren was low-key but audible in every room. Duke had also installed revolving red lights from police cars around the place to add to the siren. Overkill.
Randy and Howard showed up just as a heavily armored Humvee approached the hill. I don't know why they have to drive those things. The gas mileage sucks big time. The cameras showed several more armed vehicles parked down the hill, probably waiting for word before coming in. I got an idea, so I returned and handed my gun to a startled Sarah. "Go along with everything I say and do, okay?" She nodded as I stood back from the door, leaning against the doorjamb. See, I'm harmless.
Mason shot me a look. "What are you up to?"

"I just read the guy, and I think we can do this without bloodshed. So go along with me, okay?" He frowned but nodded anyway, joining the men at the door to welcome our visitor. An aging, heavily overweight man dressed in dessert fatigues with an unusual amount of medals and bars (on fatigues?) slowly approached the steps with his hands raised. Oh, yeah, this was going to be fun.
"Just take it easy, folks, I come in peace. My name is General Ustes F. Widdlemier (you have GOT to be kidding me), commander of the New Virginia City Minute Men Battalion of North America". (Huh?) He hitched up his pants, so they fit more snugly under his hanging belly. Then pulled out a handkerchief and wiped the drool from his chin.
"Is this guy for real?"
"Are you kidding me?"
I was standing around listening to this and wanted to laugh so bad it hurt, the not laughing part.
"Hide the guns except for one. Duke, pull out that old Remington .22 you got for gophers. Watch what you say. He may be bugged or plant bugs while he's here, which I hope to God isn't long." Mason whispered while everyone ran around

doing just that. Once Randy was armed with the rifle, we invited the General inside. We offered him a seat in the stuffed chair beside the fireplace, and he refused, opting to stand in front of the fire for better effect. Spreading his legs and trying to clasp his hand behind his back, he tried to look important and failed miserably.

Mason looked at me and raised his brows. Okay, showtime.

Smiling because I couldn't do otherwise, I pulled out a Cuban cigar I'd found Duke hiding from Sarah earlier. I was going to tease him with it later but found it served a better purpose now.

"Here you are, Sargent, you just let me light this for you."

As I searched for something to light the cigar, everyone was trying to close their mouths, and the General was stuttering, "That's General, little lady, and I thank you for the kind gesture, but I had to quit smoking due to my health, you know?" No fatso, I don't.

"Well, that just a crying shame for a critical, disguised man such as yourself to have to forgo such a time-honored tradition as a fine cigar, Major. Okay, just let us get you a cup of coffee to make up for it.

"That's General, sweetheart (gag), and I would be honored to accept a cup of coffee; then, maybe we can talk for a spell," I swear he was drooling with the thought of the coffee.

Sarah rushed to get his coffee while he examined us like we were fine horses to be bought. I noticed the sweat that began to bead on his forehead and knew it wouldn't be long before he began to sweat profusely. That was a nice fire we had going.

We stood around and smiled stupidly at him until Sarah returned with the go-cup, capped and ready. If he noticed the implication, he never let on. Thanking her with a nod, he sipped the coffee, and a look of surprise crossed his face.

"Mighty fine, coffee, ma'am. I haven't had a good cup of joe in ages." He took another drink and seemed to remember what he was doing here. He looked around for a place to set the mug and finally turned and put it on the mantle. The back of his shirt was sweat-soaked. I heard Sarah stifle a laugh, and Howard coughed several times before we all managed to get hold of ourselves.

"Now," he said, wiping his sweaty palms on his pantlegs, leaving dark, wet stains, "if you ladies will excuse us, we men need to conduct some serious business."

Mason started to say something, so I jumped right in. "Oh, no, sir, we sure can't do that cause we are democrats here, and we all decide what to do. Ain't that right, sweet cheeks?" I said, snuggling right up under Mason's arms.

"That's right, private Whistlestop, we are one big happy family here. Isn't that so snuggle bottom?" Sarah said to Flynne, who looked ready to bolt out of the room.

General Idiot fought the impulse to correct her or order us from the room and finally decided to accept defeat. Something I'm sure he is not familiar with.

"Well, now, we have been monitoring your compound for several weeks (that all?), and we've seen the struggle (?) you've had to endure. It's a tough world out there nowadays, and we were of a mind to suggest, and I mean to suggest, that you all move into the fort with us while a platoon of men station themselves here to ensure the safety of this outpost."

"Oh, but Captain Ulysses, we're just fine here. Isn't that right, baby cakes? We had a guy here that did all kinds of things to keep us safe. Like those mines in the road." I turned to Randy, who looked like he had swallowed his tongue. "What's

those mines called Randy? Clay things or something, I can never remember, but they go off if the ground even shakes a smidgen. Why I swear, sometimes I'm afraid to sneeze."
He quickly glanced outside and then back at us. "Well, when we heard you were coming, we shut them off right quick cause we ain't had company for ages...well, not living people anyway." I turned to look at Mason, who was red from suppressing laughter.
"There are missles lined up on the cliff behind us, and several trailers along the road are full of live zombies, if you can call them that, and if we hit a switch, a door opens, and hundreds of zombies know its lunchtime. The trailers are all wired, so if someone tries to climb over them, they explode too." I leaned forward and whispered, "The lodge is wired to explode. Ain't that the smartest thing you ever heard? If someone kicks us out, and the code isn't reset every night, the place will go POW!..." I'm throwing my arms around wildly, "...and blow everything all to hell!" I sat back, very pleased with myself.
"He's dead now, the guy who did all this stuff, but he left the reset instructions somewhere around here. The guys won't tell me cause, well, I don't

think they trust me. Don't you think so too, Corporal?"

He was pale and sweating profusely. His eyes jumped from one of us to the other.

"You'll have to excuse Lily here, General. She gets to talking sometimes and doesn't know when to shut up. Your 'suggestion' that we move sounded good, but we are settled here and have the security firmly in hand. There are some safeguards..." I started to open my mouth, but he put his hand over it. I grinned behind it. "...that we are confident would repel any intruders that attempted to overthrow us. But we do thank you for the kind invite." I nodded at the General and batted my eyes, Mason's hand firmly planted over my mouth.

He must have realized he wasn't going to be able to talk us into leaving, so he walked to the door, where Howard handed him his coat, and I gave him his coffee.

"Just honk when you get to the gate, sir, and I'll open it for you; otherwise, it will...."

"Explode, yes, I know." He looked at each of us in turn and then directly at me. "Young lady, you are either the smartest person I have ever met or the stupidest, but I do know one thing for sure. I hope never to see you or your friends again". Pulling his hat down tightly, he turned to open the door and found Randy holding it open with a smile. Making a funny noise, he stomped out to his humvee, nearly landing on his ass on the slick bottom step.

He honked the horn loudly and long when he arrived at the gate, and Duke took his time activating it, which we all knew was driving the general crazy. Then all the humvees waiting patiently on the road turned around and followed him back to New Virginia City, wherever that is.

"Well, sweetcheeks, I think that went over very well, especially the lodge being wired to blow if the explosive device isn't reset every day. Now, let's check for bugs, then see if the one we put on him is working properly." Then he gave me a mouthwatering kiss, smacked me on the ass, and walked away.

Everyone else hugged me and congratulated me. Well, Lily, anyway.

CHAPTER 18

It'd been two weeks since General Nincompoop visited. Duke tuned up the six-foot, remote-controlled, stealth attack toy helicopter and dogged his company's retreat for a good five miles before we started to relax.

We listened to their conversations from the bug Randy placed on his coat for several days after he left. The idea that the lodge was set to explode if the detonator wasn't reset every night bothered them more than anything. They were insulted that we thought no one could if we couldn't have it. I thought it was a great idea. If not, in reality, it seemed to work as make-believe.

Leaving the New Virginia City Minute Men to Duke, I decided to go hunting with Flynne, Mason, and Howard. Duke's new camera on the top of the phone tower mountain spotted a herd of elk in the next valley. There were several bulls, and that's what we needed. We were tired of chicken and needed another crop of em before we ate up all our egg layers.

Melody was plodding around the house, looking about as miserable as anyone could when they were about to give birth. According to Joe, she ate and slept better after all she had been through. The nursery was finished, the delivery room prepped, and everyone had practiced. We were waiting for her. She followed Flynn to the door to say goodbye, which seemed to please him. She was trying to bundle him up against the cold, but it wasn't that cold today, so I could see him shedding some of it as soon as we were out of sight of the lodge.

I needed to practice with the crossbow anyway, so the first place we headed was the 'smurf' garden. There were just two more in the ravine, so I shot them. I don't know where they're coming from. They weren't getting into the compound, so I had no problem with it. We had discussed it to death, and we just can't come up with an explanation. We were going to be busy come spring hauling those things out of the creek. When I shot the first one, a loud thunk surprised me until I realized they were frozen. I shuddered anyway, and when I turned and saw Mason watching me, I just

shrugged. Some things just never got easier.
The air was cold to my nostrils when I breathed in too hard, and the tips of my ears got cold fast until I pulled the cap down lower on my head. Walking with snowshoes wasn't as bad as I thought it'd be. I had to tighten the straps a couple of times before they felt right, and then I could move pretty well. I wouldn't want to run in the things, but walking worked. We could've used the snowmobiles, but the less noise, the better. I knew we would see more game in the valley than above in the higher parts of the mountains. Most of the bigger animals stay in the lower parts of the hills, where it's not as cold, and there's more food and less snow.
We stopped once and ate a handful of nuts and drank some water. Staying downwind, we slowly approached a small herd of elk. With hand motions, I indicated I would take the cow on the left, and the others showed which ones they would shoot. I had traded my bow for a 30.06, and as I went down on bended knee, I set up my shooting stix, a stick with a vee at the top where I could rest the gun's barrel. They get heavy even if I hold them up for any time. We figured we were about 300 yards from them when we all fired. One bull and three cows dropped. Then we ran over and

began field dressing them.

The heads were removed after they were gutted and then quartered, leaving the ribcage behind because of the gristle and fat. We did take the tenderloins before we went, and the lower legs were removed, leaving us with most of the meat. We were in a bit of a hurry with the noise, the shots, and the fresh meat, and it was a toss-up on whether we would get walkers or wolves. We quickly loaded the sleds and began the trip back. It started to get colder closer to afternoon. The mountains were throwing shadows, and it was measurably colder in them. The going was slower, pulling the sleds up the small hills with the added weight. Mason stayed behind me most of the way, then offered to take my sled.

"Back off, he-man, I can handle it." I huffed and puffed, trying to catch my breath. I don't know why it was such an issue, but there you go. I didn't need to prove anything to Mason, so I tried to prove something to myself. Whatever that was.

"Here, eat something," he said, handing me a granola bar. We found a pallet of the damned things, and whenever I turned around, someone tried to feed me the stale stuff.

"You're a bit of a mother hen," I told him, not sure

whether to be irritated or not.
"And you're grumpy when you're tired and hungry." He removed a bottle of water from his pack, drank heavily, then gave it to me. We looked around us at the mountains as we rested. In the distance, we heard a wolf howl and knew we needed to get home before he decided it would be easier to take our meat. Putting my back into pulling the sled, we continued on our way.
It was almost dark by the time we arrived. Placing the sleds with the elk in one of the cabins to protect them from predators until we could take care of them, we trudged back to the cabin, too tired to think straight. The welcome smell of ham and beans with the added enticement of homemade bread embraced us as we opened the door, and my stomach growled like an old bear.

A week later found us preparing for Christmas. The tree was nearly hidden behind the many gifts, with the smaller ones stuck in the branches. The smell of pies and bread baking kept us all in a constant state of hunger. Christmas music was playing, and someone was always singing or humming along. Joe and Flynn followed Melody around like puppies, worried she might drop that baby on the floor.

The day before Christmas found ourselves arguing about Christmas Eve. I was always told that Christmas started on Christmas Day and none of this Christmas Eve stuff. It seemed we were evenly divided about the issue, which made it even harder to decide. After supper, we decided if some of the 'eve' people wanted to open their presents, then go ahead, but us die-hards were waiting till Christmas day. It was decided when Melody's water broke unexpectedly while getting up from the couch.

I thought Flynn would lose his mind, and Joe wasn't much better. I wondered if Melody would have to deliver this child herself when a white-faced Joe took a deep breath, escorted Flynn, carrying Melody, into the clinic, and closed the door softly behind Lacy and Sarah. The rest of us just pretended to watch "It's a Charlie Brown Christmas" with Mandy while ignoring the moans coming from the other room. The movie ended, and Mandy removed the disc and turned the tv off. I hugged and kissed her goodnight and sent her to her dad.

The moans continued till midnight when they became louder, occasionally substituted by a scream. I know just from the sounds I heard that there was no way I would ever have a child. Nope, no way.

Soon the sounds reached a peak and then quieted, followed by the sound of a newborn's cry. Mason finally got his nerves in order and sat with me while we waited. I thought he would pass out by the time the baby cried, and his face told me he was glad he'd toughed it out.

"No. Don't even think about it. It ain't happening, so get that stupid look right off your face this instant, or you'll never touch me again. These panties will stay on."

"Stupid look? Don't you hear that? Isn't that the sweetest sound you've ever heard?" He went to the door to listened closer, pressing his ear to the door.

Trying to distract him, I asked, "Mason, tell me when that child's birthday is."

He looked confused for a second, then he broke out in a laugh. "I'll be damned, oops, I mean danged, hanged, whatever...a Christmas baby. Hot dog, Randy, we got us a Christmas baby."

"You didn't didn't have a damn thing to do with it, so stop bragging," Randy said, strutting up to Mason and pressing his ear to the door. They were

nearly nose to nose and grinning like they'd won the lottery. However, they almost fell on their faces when an exhausted Flynn opened the door and walked out, holding a small bundle in his arms. He was grinning too, and when he pulled the cover back a bit, and we saw that baby, all thoughts flew from our minds. Yeah, she was beautiful and bald. She looked a little like Flynn.
"Congrats, dad. Now maybe you'll leave that poor girl alone."
"She's resting now, but she did a great job. I wanted to show her off while they cleaned Mel up and get her comfortable. I don't think I ever want to go through something like that again, though."
"Yeah," I said, touching that satiny, soft newborn skin, "I can see where it could be tough on you." He frowned at me, knowing the sarcasm was somewhere, then gave up and smiled at the guys before returning to Melody. Soon an exhausted Lacy and Sarah stepped out and quietly shut the door. Randy and Lacy headed upstairs arm in arm while Sarah took care of something in the kitchen. Mason took my hand and led me upstairs to my room. We quietly got into bed, where I snuggled against his back. He took my hand, kissed my palm, then clasped it tightly against his chest.

Soon we were both asleep.

A loud, piercing scream startled us into falling out of bed only to jump up and start for the door. Another scream woke us up and barely stopped me from flinging open the door and running downstairs, naked. It was Christmas morning, and Mandy had just gotten up, discovering the many presents with her name on them. Leaning against the door, trying to catch my breath, I heard a thump and turned in time to see Mason hopping around the room with one leg in his pants and then falling on his butt. Well, this bodes well.

I ran to the bathroom and tried to close the door, but he beat me to it. We smiled at each other, kissed, then softly whispered "Merry Christmas" before climbing into the shower together. Warm water and soap handled by a loved one makes for a very nice Christmas present.

I had a friend that used to wrap all the gifts he gave with the Sunday funny pages. I thought it was a great way to recycle, and after viewing all the wrapping paper strewn about the lodge, I had to agree. Of course, the funny pages have gone the way of most humans, and wrapping gifts with the funnies would never have caught on anyway.

Coffee was calling my name, and I guess no one

could open presents until everyone was present. I could have had a lot of fun with that but didn't want to deprive Mandy, so I strolled into the great room and found a chair.

Duke was the official gift presenter in green tights, boots, shirt, and pointed hat. I didn't know we needed one, or I would've suggested Mason for the job. *Very funny, Brat. I'll remember that come to Valentine's Day.*
Stay out of my head, Meathead. There's still Easter. How he looked at me then reminded me of the shower, and I blushed, making him laugh.

I allowed Duke to pile my gifts on the floor while I quietly sipped my coffee and relaxed. When he kept piling them up, I started to get concerned. Where did all these come from, for Pete's sake? I started looking around the room and saw everyone was waiting for me to start opening them up. Sighing, I put down my coffee and started working on them.

The gifts indicated that they had all gone out of their way just for me. A beautiful western shirt made by Sarah and a matching beaded necklace made by Lacy were followed by a gorgeous handmade jewelry box by Flynn. Randy had painted a beautiful portrait of Lacy, and another of

Mason dressed the way he was when we met. There was even a pet store in the background. Howard had fashioned an antique brass belt buckle from a 1960s Ford Galaxie 500 XL Emblem. Where he got it is a mystery. I was in tears when I got the thing out of the beautiful wooden box he had 'wrapped' it in. The picture I'd admired of Mandy's was wrapped in a Barnwood frame by a child. I oohed and aahed appropriately and hugged the stuffing out of her. Sissy presented me with a piece of barn wood she had burned. "Knock before entering." It was for my bedroom door. Duke made a clock out of a computer motherboard which was so outrageous it was beautiful. I didn't know Joe made dreamcatchers, and everyone received one with different feathers and beads. Melody made a group of pictures of each member, which was priceless, and Sam had made me a rag rug for the floor next to my bed.

It was a wonderful day. Dinner was outstanding, with a giant ham gracing the table with vegetables, breads, pies, cakes, and candy. Melody managed a light dinner while we tried to stay away from Davy, our Christmas baby. She slept, mostly, but that didn't stop us from staring

at her. Lacy took a million pictures, and everyone played with her. It was too good, and I loved Christmas for the first time in a very long time. Lying next to Mason that night, I thought of all the wonderful people I had somehow managed to surround myself with. Mason opened the blinds so we could see the stars, and when he returned to bed, he put something on my stomach. I sat up and gently opened the tissue-wrapped package. A crossbow of silver with a silver arrow on a silver necklace was nestled in the white tissue (I discovered the next morning in the light of day that the tissue was toilet tissue). It was the most beautiful piece of jewelry I'd ever seen.
"Tomorrow, I have a real surprise for you, but it's not for Christmas, just something I wanted to get you." He kissed me on the nose, then turned off the light so we could watch the stars. He held my hand as I slipped to sleep, and before I was lost to the night, I heard, "I love you, JD."
Didn't I?

To be continued

Made in the USA
Middletown, DE
09 October 2022